The Ladies Compartment

Extraordinary Tales of Ordinary Women

Inspired by true events

Parminder Kaur Sharma

ISBN:978-93-5493-258-8

I dedicate this book to the corona warriors. We can never repay you.

SURPRISE !!!

FREE BONUS GIFT !!

You get Free Bonus Chapters along with their Hindi Translations from the book -

FROM MONKEYING TO PARENTING

Check Out : https://bit.ly/3B1WNa7

CONTENTS

Acknowledgement

"Expect Nothing, Appreciate Everything"
-My Father's Mantra

I would like to thank each and every person I had met and each and every experience I had so far in my lifetime, good or bad, because they all attribute to, what I am today and thus this book.

However, there are people without whom this book could not have been possible.

First of all, I am grateful to my parents for all that they have done and are still doing for me and especially to my father, for giving me the love of words and writing and my mother, for giving me the habit of always doing something constructive, via their DNA.

To my Bhabhi for supporting me in all my endeavours, be it my running, blogging, my first book and now this; and to Bhaiya for bringing Bhabhi to my life.

To my mother-in-law for supporting me

throughout the making of this book and for understanding me, not being able to give her that time and attention while this book was taking shape.

To my life time support, my husband for being with me through thick and thin, always.

To my kids for teaching me new life-lessons and helping me become a better person each day.

To my friend, the iron lady- Sonali Kohli for patiently listening to me all through the making of this book.

To my mentor and guide for life, Sh. Parveen Ved ji for being the lighthouse for me. He always shows me the right path whenever I am stuck.

To my book coach Ms. Sweta Samota. Her guidance has helped me a lot in improvising not only as a writer but as a person as well, by being more focused and effective.

And, last but not the least, You - my reader, for selecting, reading (and hopefully reviewing too!) my book.

Thank You.

Introduction

All living beings need energy to strive. The plants get their energy from their roots and we humans derive our energy and our strength from our cultural roots, our history. When talking about strength I cannot think of anyone else than Devi Sita.

Devi Sita was the epitome of courage, strength, character and patience. Her life was full of struggles and she faced each one of them with immense bravery and fortitude to become a perfect daughter, a perfect wife, a perfect mother and above all a perfect human being.

If Shree Ram is worshipped as Maryadapurushottam, Shree Sita definitely is MaryadaStriottam.

We are blessed to be descendants of such divine personalities.

But we also have the option for choosing our source of power, it can be Ram or Ravan, Sita or Swaroopnakha, the choice is all ours.

When life threw them challenges Vaidehi,

Tarini, Bhavya, Ramaa and Bhaumi, they made their choices and got their inner strength from the divine supreme power.

I bow to Shree Narayan, residing in the hearts of all of us.
I bow to Shree Lakshmi, strengthening each one of us.

"Har Nar Main Narayan,
Har Nari Main Lakshmi."

THE LIFE MACHINE

The Noida City Centre Station like any other terminal station is always crowded but today it was different for many reasons.

The platform was less crowded today. I was reading a book, putting my waiting time to some good use. I glanced at the display that blinked '07:00' against my train's name and I went back to my book.

After the promised time, the train arrived. Being a daily commuter, I knew my exact spot to stand to have my favourite seat in my favourite compartment. I temporarily assigned the job of a bookmark to my index finger and closed the book. Today, being Saturday, my killer seat-grabbing instinct was put on hold and I easily managed a quiet corner in the compartment. My fellow passengers also settled and the train resumed its motion. I released my finger from its assignment and opened my book.

Everything was going as usual, till I heard that peculiar voice.

"Hmm, good choice of book," a deep echoing voice said to me. I gazed all around but could not locate the source of it.

"What? Can you hear me?" the voice seemed as surprised as me.

I stood up with a jerk. My co-passengers looked at me as if I was about to deliver a baby right in front of them.

"Don't act weird. Chill and sit back."

It was terrifying now. I wondered if I was having hallucinations or did I land up into a haunted compartment?

"Ha ha ha... I am not a ghost."

I was scared to hell. I rushed towards the door to get out as quickly as possible. My co-passengers were enjoying their show. One was smiling sheepishly at me and another one was rolling her eyes. I was puzzled. Why were they not able to hear this strange voice?

"Even I am surprised. You are the first one who can hear me," the voice was readily available to answer my questions.

"Who...who are you... let me go..p... please let me go." I pleaded though no one had caught my hand and no one was stopping me to go anywhere. Maybe that's the default reaction in a scary situation like this.

"Relax, don't panic." The moment someone tells you not to panic, the intensity of it rises exponentially. At least the same holds true in my case. "There is nothing to be scared of. Please take your seat". This time it spoke authoritatively.

With no scope of any cooperation from my neighbours, I decided to abide by it. I sat hesitantly and in a meek voice, asked it again, "Who are you?"

"I am your compartment."

"C...compartment?" My voice was trembling with fear.

"Yes, I am the ladies' compartment and you do not need to utter words to talk to me. I can read your mind". This made it even scarier.

"How could it be true? Compartments don't talk."

"Yes, generally they don't but I am special".

"Special?"

"Yes, I am special for two reasons. One- because I am dedicated to the most courageous creature God has ever made, the women," this statement played a small role in boosting my confidence and I straightened my back in reflex, "and second, you already know- I can read people's minds." The little boost I had a nano-second before, vanished altogether. "I can travel through the lives of the people."

"What do you mean?" The cocktail of my emotions was now having more surprise than fear.

"Um...just like a time machine, that travels through time, you can think of me as a 'Life Machine' that travels through lives". The voice turned a bit friendly now or maybe the casualness by which it spoke to me, made me feel so.

"And, why do you think you need to do this... the 'Life machine' thing?"

"Oh, it is so enriching."

"Enriching?" I was questioning every word it said, but then this was not an ordinary conversation happening.

"Yes, indeed. Every time I peep into someone's life, I feel they deserve a big applause. The bravery rewards they give you on your Republic Day need to expand its scope." From friendly, it now moved to be motivating. I was now enjoying the conversation.

"Do you really feel these ordinary-looking women can have something in their lives to enrich someone?"

"I almost daily experience their struggles and how they fight against all odds."

Despite it trying to be convincing, I find it hard to

believe. After all, these were just ordinary women, who are part of the daily crowd. If I look at my mundane routine, from home to office and back to home, it's running in an automated mode. I have done nothing in my life that can motivate others. Ok, maybe feeding those pigeons that I do, outside the station counts for that motivation, but enriching is definitely an overstatement.

"Hmm, you need to see it for yourself to believe". I recalled that it can read my thoughts. "Let me take you on one such journey. Are you ready for it?"

I looked around and then at my book. I had some other plans for this travel but it's not every day that you hit into a vehicle that can talk. So, it was worth giving a shot.

"OK, I am ready."

"That would be fun. I have never done this with an accomplice."

"What exactly do I need to do?"

"Nothing much. If you can hear me, I can probably let you experience my journey, where you will feel as if they are telling their stories to you."

"But is it fair, peeping into someone's life?"

"People tend to put on a tough face for the outer world but inside their pain is oozing out. It's only with these pain-stricken women that I can connect, who want to be heard. I don't think it's unfair to feel someone's pain. So, do you want to check this out?"

This time, I carefully observed my co-passengers. "OK, how about that girl, sitting in a blue salwar kameez?" I referred to a woman who was probably in her early 30s. She was carrying a brown tote and was sitting with eyes closed and earphones plugged.

"Her name is Vaidehi."

"What? Can you know her name?"

"C'mon, seriously! How many times do I need to tell you? I am about to show you her whole life and you are shocked, just to know her name?"

My Maths teacher in the third semester was the last person, who made me feel so dumb.

"I am asking you one more time. Do you think you are ready for it?"

Enough humiliation for the day. "Yes, I am."

"OK then, sit back and close your eyes."

It was truly a 'Time Machine' type thing. As if I was

transported to her life, as if I became she. I became Vaidehi.

"When deprived of something, find a higher purpose."

VAIDEHI

I was a chatterbox in college. I could speak nonstop on any topic, whether or not I had any idea of the context, and that made it very easy for me to mingle up with my friends or even strangers.

It's the same me but now I avoid seeing people. I avoid talking to even my close friends or relatives. That's why I did not want to go to the party that day. Had my better half Aman not insisted, I would never have been there and could never have found the true purpose of my life.

It was the wedding anniversary of his colleague. I had met the couple on a few occasions before. They were hosting a lavish party in a countryside resort. I find these fancy parties a waste of time and money, both for the host and the guest. The resort was over-decorated for the purpose. In fact, the purpose itself was overrated. There was a big banner at the entrance that read "Kshitij and Romi Welcome You" below their life-sized portrait. Wasn't it obvious? We were invited and I was personally insisted for coming. I expected this welcome but that need not be put in writing. Again, a sheer waste of money.

As expected, and as promised we were welcomed.

"Hey Aman, late again?"Kshitij said.

"Arey sorry yaar, you know the city traffic." Aman gave his not-needed explanation. The traffic was smooth and we had come eleven minutes before our planned time.

"I know. Namaste Bhabhi. I am so glad you came." After exchanging the unnecessary pleasantries, he called his wife. "Romi, see Aman and Bhabhi have come," as if she could not see for herself. What he actually meant was to take me towards the ladies corner so that he can show Aman where the drinks were being served.

“Come Vaidehi,” she smiled and showed me the way to the area dedicated to us.

Aman was standing in another corner laughing amongst his friends, each one of them holding a glass. While our corner, as expected, had a bunch of kids playing.

Some kids were snatching the cold drinks of others, despite having an array of all coloured sugar-loaded ones over the counter, leaving the victim kids to cry at the peak of their hoarse voice. Some were licking the lid of the cornetto while the cone was melting away and the rest of them were enjoying the bliss of tearing off the over-done decoration. There were some learned members too, the teens and the pre-teens who were glued to the smartphones. I sometimes wonder, if we call these gadgets smart, what would they be referring us as, dumb humans, maybe?

The ladies were doing their rounds of laughter in chorus, with varying pitch and frequency. Every other moment a sharp voice of one of the moms interrupted the laughter marathon, instructed her kid, and seconds later got merged to it.

Romi spoke the names of the chorus members one by one to me and it vanished my mind as soon as I heard them. Some of them I already knew and the rest I hardly cared to know. The round of selfies was simultaneously in full swing with all combinations of weird faces and poses.

"So, how is Rohan doing? He is in 8th standard na?"one of them asked the other, scanning her freshly captured pout on her phone.

"He is in 9th now. I have put him to SN IIT coaching. It's a really good center."

Coaching from class 9th itself? Why didn't you start in nursery?

"How is Ananya, is she liking her new school?" The second lady asked the third, gulping her fourth round of paneer tikka.

“Anya, her name is Anya,” the lady corrected her opponent with a caustic attitude. “She badly misses her school back in the States.”

Following the pattern, now it was her turn to ask another child-oriented question to the fourth one.

The pattern was though broken when a question cut me sharp as a razor, “How old are your kids?”

How was I assumed to have them just because I was married for some number of years that fell into their self-prescribed cut-off? I hated answering such mindless questions.

I spilled some coffee over my dress purposely, pretending to be done by mistake. I could be overconfident of my acting skills, but it was better to take this chance than to answer that stupid lady.

“Oh, excuse me. May I..? Where is the washroom?” I asked Romi and escaped the circus.

I took a deep breath of relief in my solace in

the restroom and my jawline also felt relaxed from those fake smiles. I took out my phone from my bag. I had been tagged in some weird posts. #feelingjoyful #AnandaResort #RomiKiParty.

A smashing sound somewhere from the backside caught my attention. It seemed some plates fell off. A heavy male voice was shouting at someone, perhaps scolding the one who dropped those dishes. I resumed my 'smartphone-dumbhuman' time.

The backdrop again made some noise. This time it was a trembling meek crying. I had this strong urge to check on this voice. I came out of the restroom and found my way to the back of it, tracking the source of the noise.

It was at the far end, in a dimly lit corner. It didn't even feel like part of the same resort which was busy with unnecessary celebrations. I saw some poorly dressed kids there, washing the dishes along with some men.

"Hey, who are these kids and what are they doing here?" They looked at me and went back to their job as if I was that sales-girl selling some washing powder in the bus. I visualised an imaginary banner here – 'We do not welcome you.'

I repeated my question and one of them uttered some words in his own dialect and a better-looking man appeared from inside.

"Kya madam, what's the matter?"

I asked the same question and got the same response. That same sales-girl feeling. I went back and shared it all with Romi to which she casually remarked, "Oh, they must be with contractors."

Did I appear so dumb to her? Of course, I knew they were with them.

"How could they use children as labour?"

"Arey Vaidehi, they all do it."

"But they should not be doing it and we should not be allowing it!"

She gave me such a bad look which by definition could be treated as a smile as her lips moved in an upward 'U' direction, but made me feel even worse than that sales-girl.

I went straight to Aman and told him about it. His reaction was somewhat better.

"That's very bad, but what can be done?"

"C'mon we can stop it. You should raise this with Kshitij."

He, on my insistence, spoke to Kshitij. If I can come to this insane circus on his insisting, this was not much to ask in return.

They both shared some talks and nods and they went out of the hall. I followed them to that far end where I saw those kids. Kshitij was giving some instructions to the contractor. I stepped close to listen.

"This is not acceptable. You can't bring kids to work here. What will people think of me?"

Seriously, was this his concern? His reputation? Anyways at least he did something, better than his wife who was busy playing those stupid game of baseless questions. I was sorry for Kshitij for having a ringmaster as a wife and the irony was, he was celebrating it.

The kids got up and followed one man in the other direction. I patted my back for being able to rescue these kids from the labour.

I wished I could give them something to eat before they leave but knowing my hosts, I dropped the idea. One of them, a girl maybe around eight or nine, turned back to look at me. I could not take my eyes off her till she merged into that dark corner of the street.

The party continued with its hustle and bustle as if nothing had happened. It hardly mattered to them who were the people running the show behind this decorated fake world.

My trauma finally ended and we left for home. Aman was proud of me for having raised the issue. Even I was thankful to him for letting Kshitij intervene.

The next weekend we went out for dinner. Earlier these dinners were for a change but now had become a routine with nothing else better to do. They came as a good distraction from our otherwise empty lives.

Aman and I were deeply in love but there was something missing in our lives. No matter how much we tried to convince ourselves that we two were enough for each other, we knew we both wanted to expand our love. Being a patient of PCOS, I was not able to conceive for the past five years and I was still waiting for my family to be complete, for my own self to be complete.

We had been trying treatments from all branches of science and belief, but all in vain. Though Aman never made me feel any less but when I noticed him patting some young kid at a park or smiling at some child in the other car while driving, I could feel his void yet could do nothing.

I laid back on my seat with my eyes closed. The car stopped and with the knocks at the window, I could guess it must be the traffic signal. I looked out and was surprised to see a girl begging, carrying an infant in her lap.

“Aman, see. Isn’t she the same girl?” I said without taking my eyes off her.

“Which girl?”

“Arey this one, the girl standing.”

“Arey baba, which same girl are you talking about?”

Before we could reach any conclusion, the signal turned green and he moved forward to leave.

“Wait wait wait” I slid the windows down and peeped out of the window. She was gone within seconds.

“What? What’s the matter?”

“She was the same girl I saw at the party.”

“You could be mistaken. These kids look all the same. I mean their upkeep, their clothes.

“No, I am sure. I remember those eyes.”

I wanted to track her but Aman would not have liked the idea.

Those eyes couldn’t let me sleep that night. As if they wanted to tell me something.

The next day after Aman left, I took my scooty and went to the same crossing. These people generally have designated areas where they could be located. That's what Madhur Bhandarkar told us in his movie, Traffic signal. I waited and kept strolling there for more than two hours but there was no sign of any beggar or vendor. Watching that movie four years ago seemed so futile today.

It took me ten minutes to reach the place but going back was a thirty minutes' drive, owing to traffic adding more to my frustration. It was now the pick-up time for kids from school, so school buses and all, added to the chaos. Also, the auto-rickshaws and ice-cream vendors lined up from nowhere.

I was making my way out of this mess when my bulb finally lit. The vendors and their associates come out at the right time and not just when some Bollywood-motivated jerk decides to find them.

The car behind me kept honking for seven and a half minutes when I took the sharp u-turn.

I reached back at the signal and this time I

could find some of ‘those’ kids stopping by the cars lined up at the signal. She was not there. I signalled them and they all came rushing towards me pleading with outstretched hands.

I asked them about their whereabouts. One of the kids replied pointing towards a lane. He must be six or seven. I could not make out his exact words but he gave me the lead. I took out some chocolates from my bag and distributed it to them. They all took it, some happily, some with disappointment.

I followed the pointed lane till its end and kept roaming on the streets that led further. There were big houses and villas. I could not find any slum areas there. After spending a quarter of my fuel tank roaming pointlessly, I returned back home exhausted.

I laughed at my foolishness, at my first and failed attempt of acting Mr. Sherlock Holmes. But despite me trying to demotivate myself, I could not give up.

I went there again the next day. I was lucky, it did not take me long to see some of those kids entering my lead- the same lane, while I was standing on the other side of the signal.

My scooty made a squeaky sound as I raced it to catch up with those kids. There were four of them, hardly dressed and two of them were bare-footed. The path turned to a muddy lane and the kids stopped near the gate of a house. I parked my scooty near the turn avoiding any attention from the house-owners. The gate was rusty and the little garden outside the house was barren. The look of the house gave a quick glimpse of my own life.

A fat, dark-skinned man came out to the gate and the kids went to him. Some more kids came from inside with cloth bags hung on their shoulders, which they one by one, handed over to the fat guy. He then turned inside and the kids followed different lanes and went out.

I took out my phone and clicked the pics of the house and zoomed in to capture the nameplate affixed on the patchy boundary wall.

There was a small tea shop nearby. I went there and took a patty and a cup of tea. Impressed by my own performance of spilling coffee that evening, I decided to go for another shot.

"How are you Bhaiya?" I asked the tea vendor, acting smart. I am otherwise also smart, but at times like this one needs to act it also.

He didn't even care to look at me and was committed to rotating his kettle filled with tea in a circular motion, defying gravity.

It's since time immemorial that I have been making tea. The day when I can sieve it in a cup without spilling some drops on the kitchen slab, is yet to arrive and here he was playing so casually, with the centripetal forces acting on the tea.

"I have come here after a long time. We used to live here in that lane. That house over the corner, it wasn't built at that time. Whose is it?"

"I don't know madam." He was unmoved even by my astonishing performance.

"OK... I was asking because it is so unlike other houses. It's so deserted." I kept on trying.

He tilted his face and then nodded in negation.

Then I thought of that masterstroke, I used to play in my college days to break a nonsense conversation. This is an evergreen topic continuing for ages and you can crack conversation with anyone using this trump card.

"I heard it is a haunted house. Some people say they have seen ghosts here at night."

"Arrey nahi madam. Not ghosts but I often see some goon-types people here."

"Goons! Really? How do you know?" I confess. I over-acted at this point.

"Pata chal jata hai madam. Twenty five rupees."

Just when I was about to get some solid information, he brought his commercial interest in there. I stayed near that house for another one hour but there was no sign of any movement after that.

I came back home but I wanted to know more about that place. What was that fat guy up to? Who were those kids and why were they there?

The tea vendor had given enough fodder for my brain to keep me restless.

I spared the weekend as it was not yet the right time for Aman to know about this. My guilt of not telling him the truth tried to win over me but I knocked it on its face to make it lie down for another few days.

The next Monday morning at my planned time, I started my quest again. I went straight to that house and like the other day, stood at the corner but could not catch a very good sight this time. A mini-bus blocked the path. A name was painted on the side of the bus- ‘Sarvodaya Bal Vikas Anathalya’. I was clicking pictures of it when it started moving. I grabbed my scooty and followed it. After some zig-zag motions, the bus resumed at the main road and after around ten minutes of following the road, it took a turn towards the left and halted near a big building. The building had the same name as on the bus.

The driver came out and went inside the building. I waited for some time but nothing happened. I googled about the orphanage on my phone. Nothing substantial could surface. I decided to go inside.

It was a boxed place with no balconies. The windows were all closed with tinted glasses and the walls were dark and ugly. This one looked like a haunted house for sure, or at least suitable for the shooting of a horror movie.

I rang the bell that no one answered. I rang it again. I looked around and saw a CCTV right over my head. Such an ill-looking, un-kept place under CCTV surveillance made my doubts go stronger.

I rang the bell once again. A semi-old man dressed as a guard appeared chewing gutkha.

"Hanji Madam."

"I want to meet the manager." The term seemed out of place though.

"No manager today. All leave. You also leave." He was trying to impress me with his communication skills.

"There must be someone with whom I can talk. I wanted to offer some donation."

"Donation? Wait, madam." He picked out an extinct model of Nokia phone from his pocket and called somebody. He probably was asking his boss. He nodded his head thrice like a pendulum, leaving me wondering if it was a yes or a no. He then came near the gate and tried to open the bolt, which squeaked, when he moved to open it. It seemed stuck and was taking more than expected time to open.

He utilised this extra time in asking that stupid question, "Your baba's b'day madam?" I generally ignore such questions but here I decided to play along.

"Yes," the gate opened at once as if my answer was the password for it.

"Come, madam. I will call didi." I followed him to a room. The sight inside was even more gruesome. Black dirty walls with plaster chipping off from almost all places. Gandhiji was managing himself somehow on the photo frame dangling on a single hook. The fan of the room was contributing only to the noise.

A middle-aged lady came out adjusting the *pallu* of her georgette saree. She resembled some character from a 90's movie. I was unable to recall, but she was nowhere close to a manager or even the leave arrangement of a manager. Her hair and face looked as if she had just got up from sleep.

She opened a bill book sort of thing and forced a smile to me. "Madam kitna donation dena hai?"

I was figuring out what to do next to know more about the place. She looked at me again this time without the smile and repeated her question in English.

"Madam, what is your amount of donation?"

"Can I see the kids?" I asked.

"Mam, we don't allow outsiders to see kids. Safety issue na madam."

"OK...Can I see their CCTV footage?"

"Madam CCTV bhi nahi dikha sakte. Not allowed." This time she stared right into my eyes.

The longer I stayed there, the stronger I felt that something was going very wrong at this place but I had no idea how to find the truth.

Then I heard some giggles from the room behind that lady. The entrance of the room was covered with a DIY curtain. I could not see very clearly but could catch the glimpse of a girl sitting close to a man in a very awkward manner. The way they were sitting and giggling made me very uncomfortable. I looked back at that make-shift manager. With the clarity of context of the background scene, that movie character came clear to me. She looked exactly like a brothel keeper.

Shivers went down my spine. Was this really an orphanage or some dirty business was going on behind these ugly walls?

“Madam, kitna? Fast please.” She was turning impatient.

I opened my wallet and took out the first note that came in my hand and was about to hand it over, but I realised it was a 2000 rupee note. I looked for a better option and handed her a 500 rupee note.

She gave me a cold look collecting that note. ‘C’mon 500 is not that small amount’, my self-respect wanted to tell her but I gave priority to my self-defense rather than self-respect and turned back to leave.

“Madam, parchi to le jao. What is baba’s name?” I wanted to kill myself or her. Couldn’t she ask my name or my husband’s name or father’s name or guardian’s name even? Who asks baba’s name?

“Bobby,” I uttered a name and took the slip from her. I tried to capture every detail while going out as I was frightened to click any pictures.

I came back home and now I had enough to share with Aman. I knew he would not be very happy to know about it, but I had to tell him now.

While I was waiting for him, I tried searching about the orphanage again but could not locate any information.

I heard the beep sound of the garage door being opened. Aman had come and as was expected he was mad at me when I told him.

"Have you gone out of your mind, Vaidehi? Do you have any idea how risky this could have been?"

"I didn't know what it would lead to. I was just looking for that girl and now I can't ignore what I found."

"No, you have to ignore. We cannot do this and everyone knows there's a nexus of these child beggars."

"Aman, it's not just about begging anymore. These kids I am sure are being subjected to heinous crimes. How could I let it go?"

"Listen, I understand your concern and I respect it. But it's too dangerous. We are ordinary people. We can't fight with goons. You need to step back."

“Aman, all these years, we tried everything to have kids. I so much wanted to have my own child, whom I could carry in my arms, with whom I could play, to whom I could read story books, whom I could drop to school, and about whom I could talk to other women. When anyone talks about their children, I feel as if they are taunting me by telling their motherhood stories. I feel my life has no meaning.”

“I understand Vaidehi and I too wanted to have our family grow but I have accepted God’s wish and I have no complaints.”

“You are right, but today God has given us another chance. We can’t have our own children but we can help these children. We can save them and maybe help them to meet their parents. These could have been abducted from their homes. Think of their families. We can help them. We can do our bit at least.”

“Vaidehi…”

“Please Aman.”

He closed his eyes and went into deep

thought.

"OK. But promise me you will never go there alone and from now on won't hide anything from me.

"I promise."

He took a deep sigh.

"Give me all the details you have and all the pictures you clicked."

Aman took a close look at all the pictures and picked up his laptop. I told him I have already tried searching about the orphanage but nothing could be found.

He googled "Thomas Enclave" the nameplate of the house where that fat guy lived. I had completely forgotten about that name.

After scrolling for some time, he found an old news report, citing the illegal activities going on at the place. He scrolled down to find the reporter's name, 'Mayur Sharma, Staff Reporter, National Hour.

He checked his watch. It was 10 pm already.

“Let us call the newspaper office tomorrow.”

Aman took a day off from his office the next day. He was doing more than my expectations, as always. He called the newspaper office and asked about that reporter.

“Oh.. When did it happen? I am sorry but do you mind telling me the exact date. I am his old school friend…. Ok… ?” Aman spoke to someone at the ‘National Hour’ office. He picked up his laptop again, as the conversation ended.

“What happened? Tell me.”

“Mayur had died in a road accident,” he said, with his eyes fixed on the screen.

“Oh no!”

“That’s not all. Do you know when?” He said checking the article again. “Three days after this report was published.”

“Oh my God! This can’t be a coincidence.”

“Of course, it’s not.”

He thought of something and picked up his

phone again. “Can I have a cup of coffee?”

I heard him talking to someone while I was in the kitchen. I came back with his coffee. “Whom did you call?”

Before I could get my answer, his phone rang. I checked the name blinking on the screen- ‘Kshitij calling’.

“Thanks bro. Such a help.” He ended the call and looked at me. “Get ready.”

“May I know what’s happening?”

“I will tell you on the way. Now get ready.”

We were driving to Raja Cafe at New Friends Colony, as per the destination fed by Aman in Google Maps.

“Kshitij’s brother is a chief editor in ‘The Daily’. I called him to check if he could help us with some reliable contacts in ‘The National Hour’. We are meeting this person, Ajay. Let’s see how he can help us.” He never failed to impress me.

Ajay was a smart-looking, young guy and didn't fit my imagination of a newspaper reporter, based on what they show in movies- those boring types with checked kurtas.

"I didn't know him personally as I joined after his accident. But there is this buzz that his operation of uncovering those child traffickers cost him his life." Ajay said, sipping his cappuccino.

I looked at Aman. He felt more determined.

"So, how can they be exposed?" Aman asked him.

"They are big guns and can get anyone killed with the snap of a finger."

"But there must be some way," I asked.

"If we can have a full-blow media coverage, authorities might have to take action. But that is not going to be easy. I can use my contacts and have their channels join in for this, but we would need a face."

"What does it mean?" Aman asked.

"A whistle-blower. We can give you coverage but you will have to come forward and share your story. This can be dangerous. So, think carefully."

Aman held my hand and said, "We're gonna do this."

I was glad to see that he had no doubts about it.

"But we don't exactly have a story to share. We just have this gut feeling and we joined the dots with Mayur's article," I stated my facts.

"So, who's stopping you from creating one? You have the matter, you know the truth, now cook the story," Ajay casually added.

"Oh, yeah. I can do that." I felt excited.

"It will be her story but I will be the face of it," Aman said.

"Aman, you don't need to…"

"This is going to turn ugly. I will give the interview and no more arguments on this." Aman was in no mood to listen further.

We prepared our toolkit of some facts and some ‘to be revealed’ facts.

The interview was soon running on all national news channels and print media.

Aman was getting continuous phone calls from media agencies and from some unknown numbers too. I knew he was hiding those calls from me. It was not very late when the callers revealed themselves.

It was four days after the interview. He was on his way back home when a truck hit his car.

Some passers-by took him to the hospital and one of them called me after seeing the ‘emergency contact number’ on his I-card.

I was shivering when I saw him in hospital. He had wounds all over his face and his arm had fractured. The car was smashed so hard that it was beyond recognition.

“I am so sorry Aman. It’s all my fault. It’s all because of me. I should have been here on this hospital bed, not you. I am very sorry.”

“Relax. Calm Down. Neither of us should have been here and it’s not because of you, it’s because of those criminals and this accident proves one thing, that we are on the right track. I have called Ajay.”

“Here? In the hospital?”

Just when I was wondering what was he up to, I received a call from Ajay.

“Can you come downstairs? Some reporters want to speak to you. I looked back at Aman with tear-filled eyes and went downstairs.

A bunch of reporters with mikes in their hands were waiting for me.

The next day, Ajay informed that police raided that place. It’s owner, a local MLA, had been arrested and all the kids had been rescued.

Aman got discharged from the hospital and the same evening, we decided to see that orphanage.

I had read the statements that some of the children gave to the police. It was even grimmer than my 'made-up' version of the story. They were living in hell, being tortured and sexually exploited. I felt sick of such inhuman people. Even the girls as young as four were not spared.

We reached the place and this time I found the windows of the building, wide open. Some of the kids were playing in the verandah. Even with the weak and bruised body, they were smiling.

A young lady, much deserved to be the manager, welcomed us in.

"Hi, I am Sonal. Great Job, both of you. People like you make this world worth living."

"How are the kids doin'?" Aman asked.

"Recovering from their trauma. Some of them are in a state of deep shock. They have been sent for psychological counselling."

"I am glad they are now with you, under your safe supervision," I said.

"Well not exactly. I am associated with the

Child's Rights Commission and I am an interim arrangement here. We are looking for genuine caretakers who can take this responsibility. Do let me know if you have any references."

"What's the eligibility?" I inquired.

"No eligibility as such. The applicant needs to register with us and if the background checks get cleared, he or she can go ahead with it."

I kept mum and tried to grab Aman's reaction from the corner of my eye.

He came closer, held my hand, and spoke to her, "I have a genuine reference." He then looked at me, "Can she?"

I have been trying since I entered the place but now, I could not stop my tears.

"Of course, she can. Who else can manage this place better than her?" She said with a delighted tone, "Let me bring the papers for you and we can start the procedure right away."

We were waiting for her when I saw a face trying to hide behind the curtain and smiling at me. I went close to her. She was the same girl. I hugged her tight.

Sonal returned with the form. While I was filling it up, she too tried to utilise her time with that weird question.

“How old are your kids by the way?”

“Sonal, you too!” I said to myself.

'Announcement: The next station is Yamuna Bank. Change here for Vaishali Station.'

Vaidehi packed her earplugs and got up to leave.

She amused me with her wit and at the same time amazed me with her simplicity and extraordinary courage.

"Hmm.. So, you seem impressed!" The compartment said.

"She is splendid. Who can guess that an ordinary girl like her, chased goons and made them go behind bars and now has devoted her life to the most beautiful service?"

"We all have a purpose in our lives. All we need to do is follow our inner callings and find it."

"Also, I never realised how our casual questions, answers to which does not even matter to us, can be so disturbing for someone. I would be conscious of putting them to people from now on."

"That's nice. See you then, you can go ahead with your book now."

"Wait wait, I still have some time. Can we do it once more?"

"Are you sure?"

"Yes of course."

"OK, as you say. I love doing this whole day. Let us meet Tarini now."

"Which one is she?"

"The one sitting towards your left, in yellow top and

jeans," it pointed to a young, charming girl.

"Is she married?"

"...and here goes your commitment."

"Oops. I am so sorry. This comes so naturally to us."

"You will learn with time. Now sit back and let Tarini tell us her story."

"Home is a place where you own yourself, your life.

It's not mere possession, it's about ownership."

TARINI

I have a few faded memories of my childhood home. It was small but Mom always kept it very neat and tidy. My room was full of toys that Dad bought for me. He was planning to buy a new house soon, but I loved that home very much. Since my summer vacations of class sixth, this had become my new home.

I came here with my parents that day. My aunt, Reena Masi, the younger sister of my mother, was a different woman at that time. Me and her daughter, Agrima, were so fond of each other. She is one year younger to me but we were in the same class and bonded well and unlike my Masi she had not changed since then. I insisted that day to stay back when my parents were about to leave. I wished I had not.

They had some work and Masi offered to let

me play for some more time at her place. Dad agreed and decided to pick me up later. I had no idea that I would never be seeing them again, and would never be going back to my home again. They were coming back to pick me up when their car met with a fatal accident. They both died on the spot.

My uncle and aunt shifted to a new house the same year and since then, this became my home.

Though my school was not very far from this place, Masi got my school changed. I requested her a lot to let me continue there. All my friends were there and I did not want to leave the place where my Dad used to drop me in the morning and Mom used to pick me up in the afternoon. I even requested her to let me be in Agrima's school then, but she had planned something different. I didn't like that new school. The classrooms and washrooms were always dirty and never new classmates either.

Rohan uncle used to help Agrima in her studies, the way Dad used to help me. Uncle did help me too with some of my doubts but insisted that I should ask my teachers as they were being paid for this job.

I initially had trouble but gradually learnt to study on my own. I always scored more than Agrima and she was always happy for me. Our bond grew stronger with time.

Masi soon made me learn all the household chores. I wanted to play with Agrima after school but she assigned me daily tasks that kept me busy almost all day. Agrima tried to help me sometimes and even used to argue with her mother for me, being given so much work to do. Masi always said that with age, all girls should learn to do these household tasks. However, she never felt the need to make Agrima learn those tasks. For her, her daughter was always too young for it.

I had no complaints though. With time, I understood and accepted that they are not my parents who would pamper me as they do to Agrima. But they were giving me shelter, good food and taking care of my expenses like school fees etc.

I once overheard a conversation during

Masi's kitty party. One of her friends remarked that orphan kids like me often end up begging on the streets and it was grateful of them to take my life-long responsibility.

"After all who does it for someone else's child," one of the ladies had said.

I was indeed grateful to them, else I could have ended up in a worse place.

Time went by, we completed our schooling and I stood first in my class with ninety five percent marks. I wanted to go for MBBS. Uncle, however, was of the opinion that it was not worth wasting the time in coaching and all, as the entrance tests were highly competitive.

I was confident though and wanted to give it a try, but I did not have my say like Agrima. She wanted to pursue an MBA and the next day the coffee table was full of pamphlets of MBA coaching classes.

Masi advised me to take up an Arts course from the nearby college. I agreed to it because first, I didn't have much choice and second, it hardly mattered. Anything other than science was anyways not very appealing to me.

Soon Agrima was selected in Symbiosis, Pune and she left for her studies. I was sad but was not sure the exact reason for it. Whether it was because, I could not pursue my dream as she did or because she was leaving the home. Maybe both. Destiny had taught me to accept it and move on and so I did.

Time took another leap and I completed my graduation and also post-graduation.

I was BA, MA and Agrima, MBA. I wondered how our lives and qualifications had this similarity. Same letters but jumbled in a way that changed the entire meaning and relevance.

She came back home after five years. She got campus selected in a reputed firm and got her transfer to Noida. Despite all these years, her affection for me did not change at all. Half of her suitcase had stuff that she had bought for me. She was full of stories of the time when she bought these, with Tarun. He was the main reason that she got her transfer here, as he was also in Noida.

He was her senior in college. She took me once with her to meet him. He was a tall and handsome guy and they both made a perfect match. Their body language told, that they were deeply in love with each other.

After a few days of coming back home, she announced that they both want to get married. As expected, there was hardly any retaliation from my uncle and aunt. Tarun's parents were quite affluent and owned a chain of restaurants in Delhi-NCR. He had almost completed his internship and was about to join his family business.

Agrima and Tarun soon fixed a meeting of the families. However, uncle and aunt seemed disappointed that day when we returned after the meeting.

I asked Agrima about it but she was clear in her mind. "We want our parents to agree to this marriage but if it doesn't happen, it would be their choice. We are getting married, in either case."

I somehow liked the clarity she had of her life. On the contrary, I was always on the receiving end, simply accepting whatever life offered me.

There was the exchange of lengthy phone calls between Masi and Tarun's mother that started in the living room and ended in her room with closed doors. Marriages are by default associated with secrecy for reasons beyond my understanding.

I was cleaning the storeroom that day when Agrima came shouting, looking for me.

"Tarini ! Tarini! Where are you?"

Her excitement gave me the hint that Tarun's parents have agreed. I came out smiling, "What's the matter?"

"Guess what! You are not gonna believe it."

"OK. Now tell me. Has the date been decided?" I was signalling on her marriage date.

"It's not about me, fool. It's you. Tarun's mother wants to see you."

I had my eyes wide open. What was she talking about? How could it be me? And why was she so happy? "What are you saying?"

"Arey for Avi," she caught my bewilderment. "Tarun's elder brother. They proposed themselves."

Now, what was this? I was dazzled. My marriage was out of my thoughts and that too in a family like this? Why would they ask for me? Did Agrima make this happen?

Masi entered the room, smiling. "Yes, she is right. They themselves offered. They liked you when they saw you during our last meeting."

"Avi would be coming to India tomorrow and if you agree to the marriage, we can go ahead," Agrima added.

"Where's the question of 'if'?" They are nice people and you know them well." Masi interrupted her.

"I know them Maa, but Tarini doesn't know Avi. Even, I don't know him much. He stays in London and is coming just for marriage.

Let them meet first and then let's see."

She brought a valid point but it seemed Masi had already decided, as always. She came close to me. "We have already given our word to them and you are so lucky to be getting married to such a rich family. Your parents would be very happy today."

It was not a challenge for her to convince me on anything, even for my marriage. She could have avoided bringing Mom and Dad in the conversation.

"Where are you lost now?" Agrima took over the duster from my hand which I was still holding. "Leave this and come with me."

"To where?"

"To go shopping of course, where else?"

She bought me some pretty dresses and took me to the parlour after that. The last time I went to parlour was also with her, three years back for a cousin's wedding.

Two days later, Avi came home with his family. He was no less than his brother. He seemed smart and decent but unlike his brother, did not talk much and kept to himself. He looked at me just once when he got up from his seat during the customary *Namaste*. Tarun and Agrima on the other hand were continuously exchanging glances and smiles.

The alliance got finalised before the tea was finished. I saw Agrima signalling her mom to check with me. I nodded to her in affirmation. I had neither any reason nor probably had the choice to say no but I liked that someone was interested in knowing my decision.

After they left, she jumped in excitement and hugged me. I was happy that Agrima would be there with me and hoped Avi decides to stay back in India.

The date was finally decided. We both were getting married the same day.

I was delighted imagining my new life at my new home, with Avi and Agrima too, by my side. I was grateful for everything.

It was *Mehndi Ceremony*. The sound of dholak and ladies singing enchanted the moment. The young girls, wearing pretty lehengas, were dancing, reminding me of my care-free childhood when Mom and Dad were with me.

Agrima was also sitting beside me. She was glowing and looked beautiful. I was completely mesmerised by the moment.

The ringing of my phone caught my attention. It was a call from Avi. I picked up the phone carefully with my mehndi-applied hands. I signalled a girl standing next to me to unlock it, but before she could, the call got disconnected.

I was surprised. We never spoke and the *Namaste* we had a few days back, was the only word we exchanged. Everything happened so fast. We could neither meet after that nor did Avi make any effort to meet.

'I want to talk to you.' I read his message that was delivered minutes before his call. He might have waited for my response before calling. I was glad he was trying to connect.

I was thinking of calling him back when Masi came. "Did Avi call you?" she asked with a nervous smile.

"Yes he did, but before I could pick up..."

"Hmm.." She smiled even broader now, "No phone calls now. You can talk as much as you want after marriage," and she took my phone from my lap.

I wish I could have insisted on calling him back but I had long forgotten insisting on anything.

Finally, the wedding day arrived. I was missing my parents so much that day. I wished I could have just one chance to see them, to hug them.

I looked in the mirror. I resembled Mom that day. For the first time in my life, I felt beautiful. I wiped my tears and smiled at myself. I was about to welcome a new phase of my life and did not want to do it with tears.

The other bride entered the room. "Oh My God, look at you! You look stunning," Agrima said.

"And I need not say, you look like a princess." We both laughed and hugged each other. Her gaze stopped at my jewellery. "Why are you wearing such ...jewellery? Did Mom..."

Masi entered the room. "Um...beta, Avi doesn't like heavy..b..bulky jewellery. His mother told so and they like her simple just the way she is. Isn't she looking gorgeous?" She was stammering while speaking.

Only then I noticed her huge necklace and large earrings. It seemed so familiar. I had seen them somewhere but where? Maybe jewellery designs are all the same but no, I have felt them before. Agrima raised her hand to adjust her *mang-tikka* when I noticed her gold bangles and I recalled it. They were my Mom's.

I felt a deep stabbing pain inside me. I wanted to touch them, feel them not because of their higher monetary value, but because they were my mother's. She wore them. I remembered seeing her wearing them on many occasions. The last I remembered was during *Karwachauth*, her last *Karwachauth*.

I wished I could have at least one of it for me then I looked back at her, her smile. She was now texting someone. Her giggles told it must be Tarun. How could I even think so? She has done so much for me. She stood against her parents for me. I felt so low about myself. After all, it's just a piece of metal.

Overwhelmed with the mixed feelings inside me, I and Agrima stepped into our new lives.

During the *Grah Pravesh* ceremony, I, being their elder daughter-in-law, was asked to enter first, before Agrima. This was the first instance ever when I was given a privilege over her. I felt important and took my first step towards a better life, towards my home, at last. I wanted to forget all my pain and miseries and embrace the promise of a bright future ahead of me.

I entered a big, elegant bungalow with a huge, never-ending hall. Like in any other newly-wed-house, ladies in beautiful attires were seen at all corners. The men in shiny silk kurta pyjamas were sitting in the lawn and kids were running from one place to another.

“This is my new home,” I said to myself.

After the other new-bride-welcome rituals, we both were taken to our respective rooms. We went upstairs and I entered the room- my room.

It was a sizable room with exquisite furniture. The wardrobes were running across the whole length of the room. A luxurious bed, beautifully decorated with roses, occupied the center of the room and a sturdy, curvilinear table laid beside it. There was also a comfy leather couch at the corner near the window. The couch itself was larger than my rickety cot where I had been sleeping for so many years. I felt so out of place being at something so elegant like this.

Avi entered the room. Before I could figure out what am I supposed to do, he opened the wardrobe, took out a sheet from a shelf beneath, and spread it over the couch.

“Please sit. Please be comfortable,” he politely said, pointing towards the bed.

I complied with only the sitting part. I was not comfortable and was confused about how to start the conversation or whether I should wait for him to do it.

He spoke again, “Good Night,” and he went to sleep.

Maybe the wedding nights are exaggerated. Maybe that’s how it is and it’s good. Even I was so exhausted.

I woke up next morning and turned around to see Avi but the couch was neat and clean as if no one ever slept on it.

I stood by the large window which had small, pretty planters. I liked the fresh breeze and could feel the freshness in my life too.

I heard a soft knock and opened the door.

"Good morning," Agrima spoke in a playful tone. "How are you, madam?"

"How are you?" I tried to play her tone back."

She smiled. "Get ready, we are being called downstairs. Badi Bua ji is leaving and she wants to see us." I was surprised how she knew the stuff related to this house already. I had no idea who this Badi Bua ji was, rest aside her leaving.

We both were sitting in the living room. Tarun occasionally came and gave her company but Avi was nowhere around. This custom of 'seeing us' continued with some more relatives.

"Where are you people going?" Agrima whispered to me.

"Going where?"

"For honeymoon baba. We are going to Singapore. We are flying tomorrow."

She waited for my response and when she realised, I had no clue about it, spoke again,

"I asked Tarun also. I even asked him if we all can go together but he too had no idea of Avi's plans."

"Don't worry. Have you done your packing?" I had nothing better to ask.

"No, not yet. I am so bored sitting here. Let me see if we can..." she looked at our mother-in-law, "Mummy ji, can we now go to our room?"

"Yes, yes. Please go and take some rest." Our mother-in-law replied with a smile. Only she could have asked that straightforward question.

At dinner, she told me they are leaving early in the morning. She was too excited about it, which was obvious. I was happy for her.

Meanwhile, I was still waiting to catch some conversation with Avi, but that night too, 'good night' was the only two words we exchanged.

I woke up to Agrima's message, which she had sent at 4 am. 'We are leaving. I will keep sending you the pics. Share your plan too.' I turned back and this time I found Avi sleeping peacefully on the couch.

I got ready and came downstairs and went to the kitchen to help Maa ji.

"Arey beta wait, you cannot enter right now. We will have a '*rasoi ceremony*' to welcome you to the kitchen," she smiled and took me to the living room.

I was clueless of this ritual but was enjoying these welcome moments at every step. Maybe these steps finally take me to Avi.

"Come beta, breakfast is almost ready", she addressed someone behind me.

Avi had come and he was all dressed up. "Maa, I have my flight at 11 tonight," he said.

Flight? His flight or our flight? Was he going somewhere alone? or was it...our honeymoon?

"Why so soon, beta? You said you will stay for some time with us." Maa ji seemed to have an idea where he was going.

“You got what you wanted, right? Now let me go.” There was a hint of rudeness in his voice. He picked up some keys and went outside. I felt like asking her what's this about but then I planned to ask Avi. Afterall, I was his wife. Though till now, I had only felt as a daughter-in-law and not a wife.

He did not come till afternoon. I got anxious and picked up my phone several times but could not have the courage to call him. At last, he arrived.

He took a big suitcase lying near the wardrobe and opened it. It was almost packed up. He opened the wardrobe and was fetching something from the drawer.

“Are you going somewhere?” I had to ask about it finally.

“Yaa, I am going back, Tarini.”

This was the first full sentence he said to me that too with the mention of my name.

“Going back....?” I wanted more information.

He paused and looked at me.

“Back to my home. Back To London,” he said, flapping his hands.

“Ah.. your home…?” I was told he stayed in London but I assumed I would be accompanying him whenever he goes. I assumed now it was no longer only his home, it was mine too. It was ours.

“Yaa, I was anyways going to leave by next week but I am feeling too suffocated. I’m leaving tonight.”

I stood there with a puzzled look.

“You are already aware of everything. Now, why do you seem so surprised?” He resumed fetching things and putting them in his suitcase.

“Aware of what?” My heart was sinking now. What was this all happening?

“Don’t tell me you have not been told.”

“Told what?” I was getting desperate now.

He seemed baffled and left the room with his suitcase open. I heard him and Maa ji talking with his voice raising and Maa ji sobbing. I followed him downstairs.

Avi turned and came towards me.

“Tarini, come sit here,” he was distressed. “I was told that you have been made aware of everything and you are fine with it. Wait... I... I even sent you that message. You replied also.” He fumbled into his pocket and took out his phone, “See, you replied.”

‘I know everything about it. I will be happy to become the daughter-in-law of your house. I am OK even if you do not stay with me.’ He showed me a message sent from my number, that I never sent. How was that possible? I checked the date and time of the message. It was sent three days before at the time when Masi had taken my phone. Did she send this message to him without my knowledge, without my consent? And what was this ‘everything’ that I was supposed to know?

“I did not send this message,” I looked into his eyes.

“I can guess that. Let me tell you now,” he took a deep breath while I was losing my breath with every passing second. “You have been cheated... I... I am already in a relationship and I am going back to my home in London. We are planning to get married by this month.”

I was shell-shocked.

“Even before I came to see you, I insisted that you be told about all of this. I wanted to be sure about it, that's why I called you a day before this...this fake arrangement. But they all lied to me and to you.”

Fake arrangement?...And I thought it was a new phase of my life?

“Why? Why did you marry when ...?”

“Ask her.” he pointed to his mother. His eyes were fuming in anger. “She cannot accept a foreigner girl and wanted an Indian *Bahu* for display to the society.”

That was it? She ruined a life, just for society?

“Tarini, I am sorry. I am sorry for this betrayal that my and your family did to you.”

I was speechless.

"Please let me know if you need any help, any time from me. But right now, I need to leave," he said and went to the room which I thought was mine, was ours, picked up his luggage and left.

I felt like a fool and sat there motionless. Maa ji started giving her explanation. "Beta, I had already told everything to your family. We believed he will change after marriage. We believed you will be able to stop him but don't worry. These *firangi* girls, they can't stay with one man for long. He will come back one day."

So, was it my fault that I could not stop him? Am I supposed to wait till that … girl leaves him for me? What exactly did she mean? What exactly did she think of me? But how could I complain to her when my own aunt and uncle ditched me for life.

I wanted to talk to them. I agreed to everything they decided for me. Then why did they do this to me? I wanted my answers but how could I ignore that they took care of me, gave shelter to me for all those years.

It had been two days since Avi left and I still was not able to make sense of myself, make sense of my life. I received Agrima's message.

'Tarini, I hope you are OK. Tarun told me everything. I am coming back.'

I don't know why but I was feeling so ashamed of myself. I was afraid to face her.

She and Tarun returned back the next morning and she straight away came to my room. Tarun followed her soon after.

"C'mon Tarini. Pack your stuff. We are leaving," she hurriedly said.

"Agrima, calm down and who is this **we**?"

"You and me," she looked at Tarun as if to inform him more than me.

"Agrima, please listen to me," Tarun tried to say something.

"I don't want to listen to any of your lies," Agrima said to him.

"What are you saying? Why would you leave and where would I even go?" I asked.

"Do you think I would be able to stay with these cheats? I don't believe that Tarun wasn't aware of any of this...this bait game that they played with you."

"What bait game?"

"Tarini, our mother-in-law agreed for me on this condition of ruining your life."

"Oh my God," I said to myself. Did she really need to do this? Why could she not accept that girl and save us all from this mess?

"But I can't go back to uncle's home now," I said. I wanted to tell her that more than Avi and Maa ji it was their betrayal that has shattered me.

"I have something more to add to your agony," she said with a sigh. It seemed she had something worse to reveal. What could be worse than this? My life was already a big mockery now.

"If you think not disclosing about Avi was the only betrayal they did to you, then hold yourself tight. I have something more to add," she said.

Was she referring to those jewellery pieces of my mom that Masi gave to her instead of me? I was already over with it.

"The place that you refer to as your 'Uncle's Home', that actually belongs to you. You are the owner of that place and we all have been staying at your home. It's you who have been providing shelter to us for so many years."

"W...whhha..t What..What are you..?" I could not understand what she was saying.

"Before coming here I went to my... I mean your home to collect my degree and certificates as I have already made up my mind to leave. There in the cupboard, I found this." She handed me a bunch of papers. Those were some legal stamp-papered documents with a small photo affixed on them. I took a closer look and my heart skipped a beat. It was Dad's photo. The documents were dated June 4th 2019, the day Mom and Dad died.

I read the papers with my tear-soaked eyes. That house belonged to Dad. He purchased it that day.

The place I had been living all my life with the feeling of a tenant, a refugee was my Dad's home, my home. I lived all my life under the burden of being favoured, to be allowed to stay there, to be provided a shelter while it was always mine.

I was about to fall on the chair when Agrima held me.

"Tarini, are you OK? Please say something."

"Please...I just need to stay alone for a while," I was too shocked to react.

She understood my state of mind, as she always did and stepped back.

"OK, I am waiting in my room. Please speak to me and remember I am with you. You are not alone."

"I know. Thanks."

Someone knocked at my door at night. It must be her as she messaged a few seconds later. 'Are you OK? I am waiting for your call and please eat something. I have kept your dinner at the door."

I called Avi.

The next morning, she came rushing towards me, the moment I opened the door of my room.

"Agrima, I can't thank you more. I am leaving."

"Not you alone, we are leaving," she added.

"Listen, I would not be able to repay you for what you have done for me. Especially for letting me know my truth but now I need to sort this out on my own. I need to search for my identity. I have to do it all on my own."

"But how can I live here? We both came in together and I am not going to leave you alone now."

"Just think calmly and give Tarun another chance. I spoke to Avi last night. Tarun was not much aware of all this. My life has given me enough experience of lies and deception. I don't know whom to believe but all I have to say is, don't ruin your life in haste and I know you are wise enough to understand this."

"But where are you going and what are you going to do?"

"Bhabhi, someone has come to see you." Tarun came over.

"To see you?" She was not expecting a visitor for me but when does life do expected things.

A man in a black suit was waiting for me in the hall. I went to him and read the papers he had brought along while she was watching me desperately, trying to make out what was happening. Maa ji had joined us in the hall.

I signed them where he asked me to, after reading them thoroughly. I handed one copy to Maa ji.

"Take it Maa ji. My divorce papers."

"Divorce? How can you do this?" Maa ji asked.

"I had this exact question in my mind too. How can I? Avi helped me clear my doubts. I did not know about his relationship before marriage but he made me realise that what I could have done then, can be done even now. Kapoor ji, our lawyer, would send a copy to him also. We have mutually agreed to it. This one is your copy, just in case you need to show it to your society."

Agrima and Tarun were smiling. Agrima gave me a tight hug. I turned to pick up my luggage "Let's go Kapoor ji."

"Where are you going?" Her voice was choked.

"To my home. To take custody of my home and my life."

'Announcement: The next Station is New Ashok Nagar.'

She stood up and came near the door. She was standing next to my seat. I felt like getting up and giving her a tight hug.

"How can people be so selfish, so mean? On one hand, Vaidehi took the risk of her life to save some unknown orphan kids and here Reena cheated on her own niece. How can people stoop to such low levels?"

"Yes, there are all kinds of people around us. If we have frauds like Reena, we have people like Agrima too. Reena and her husband, Rohan might get Tarini's forgiveness but would they be able to face their own daughter?" The compartment said.

"Hats off to this girl. She happily accepted everything and I am glad she finally came to know the truth and fought her dignity back."

A girl entered the compartment from the right-most door. When a lady stood up to offer her seat, I noticed. She walked with the support of an artificial leg. She nodded her head. "It's just a few stations. I am fine." She then took out her phone and called someone, "Maa, I am coming back home," she said.

"I know, you want to know more about her," the compartment seemed as keen as me.

"Yes, indeed. The way she was dressed up carrying that handbag, I guessed she must be going to her office, like the most of us." I said.

"Actually she is coming back from her office. Come

let's see what this young woman, Bhavya has gone through."

"Your identity is not limited to your body.

You are unique. You are complete."

BHAVYA

Till three years back, I was known for my pace. I had to purposely slow down to match the speed of my friends when walking together. Now it is altogether a different story but that's my problem. I need to learn my ways to catch up.

Today was yet another morning when I started my day on time, rather before time but still failed.

The intercom of my seat rang.

"Ms Bhavya Verma?"

"Yes," I responded.

"Sinha this side. The system shows you checked in late again." Mr. Sinha had recently joined as admin incharge in my office.

"Actually.. um... I am sorry, I will take care next time." There was no point in giving an explanation. Late is late.

"It is the second day in a row. Please take office discipline seriously," he said.

"Sure."

I had just logged in to my system and he called again.

"Hi, Ms Bhavya. Sorry, I wasn't aware of ... You can have some extra time to join."

It was this pity more agonizing than him pointing me out for being late to the office by three minutes.

"Please mark me on leave today. I will join tomorrow on time," I said and took my bag to leave.

One accident changed me but more than

me, it changed the world around me. Had I missed my bus that day life could have been much simpler.

Three years have passed but that morning is still fresh in me, the last day of my college, the last day of my original, normal, pity-free life.

I was excited about the plans for the day, the party that I was about to host for my friends. I was the first and the only one in my batch to get selected and it was not just another job. It was the dream of my life. I was selected for the Indian Air Force.

I was about to reach the bus stop when I saw my bus leaving. I could have skipped it. I should have skipped it. My speed, which I always took for granted, ditched me in a way I had never expected. I failed to grab the door railing and before I could know, I laid on the road in a pool of blood.

I lost my leg to the accident. But the damage was way beyond it. The bus had overrun and crushed my life, my dreams, my dignity.

My parents were shattered for some

additional reasons. The very first thing I heard my mother saying while crying in full swing that day, “Now who is going to marry her?”

OK, I understand. I am average-looking or maybe less than average and dark-toned too. So even with my default settings, I am not a very sought-after marriage option. I know that, but this being the primary concern, that too immediately after that fateful thing, was what made me furious.

I became the centre of all the unwanted attention amongst my friends, family and relatives. They made sure I realize now how difficult my life is going to be and kept the wound afresh not only for me, but for my parents too, especially my mother. Every time my mother came to me, she would look at me and then at that ‘life-less thing’ which till now I didn’t even know existed, my prosthetic leg, and would cry uncontrollably. I had to try hard to console her. I know it’s very sick and mean to think that way, but I sometimes used to wonder, had it not been easier if it was her in place of me? Because anyways she was far more devastated than me.

The youngest member of my family, my brother Sunny, was the only one keeping the positive vibes in the house. He always motivated me and shared success stories of Arunima Sinha, who climbed Mt. Everest with her prosthetic leg, and Major D. P. Singh who is running marathons after amputation. Honestly, it did not make me feel very good about it but at least not worse.

While I was struggling with all this, my parents had geared up for their own struggle. Now it became even more urgent for them to get me married. Every other day, some aunt of mine, which till now was as non-existent to me just as my ‘new leg’, would come with a so-called very good proposal. It’s not that earlier my parents had a high expectation for my would-be groom, but now the standards were downgraded even further. Now anything that falls in the category of a boy, ready for marriage, not having any artificial replacement for any body part, was acceptable.

Some weird families would keep coming

with their weird sons, gulp on tea and samosas and would never turn up. They knew about my condition before coming, so why did they even care to come? Perhaps they wanted to see a live demo of how pathetic a life could be. Some of the 'boys' seemed double my age and for some, it took me more than three minutes to sort the components of the face. Yet, I was the one being rejected each time. I, the class topper and only one from the batch selected for IAF, had to face this rejection almost daily.

I hated going out. Adjusting my life with those pitiful looks of people was much more difficult than adjusting with my prosthetic limb. But the things at my home were worsening day by day. It was becoming unbearable now. I started applying for jobs as IAF was now obviously out of question.

I used to say it to my friends, "I would never do a 9-to-5 job. I would be flying up in the sky when you would be sulking in your boring office desks." It takes a fraction of a second to change your life. Never challenge destiny. What you say, "I would never do", it will make sure to put you in a situation where you are left with no other choice.

I got a job offer from a reputed MNC. I was 'accommodated' as much as possible, the HR guy informed during my welcome session. I hated the type of job I got and hated to go out, yet I was glad I decided for it, as it kept me away from reliving my accident daily with my family. However, I was given ample opportunities for the replay on weekends and sometimes even on weekdays.

It was on one such day.

"Take a leave for tomorrow," my mother didn't even consider the possibility of my leave getting rejected or me having some important assignment in the office for the day.

"And may I know why?" She didn't reply. The reason was obvious. "Why tomorrow? We can carry on with the drama on Sunday, or do we have any better plans for that day?"

"Bhavya please. They cannot come on Sunday. Beta, it's a very good..."

I couldn't bear those words again, "I know, it's yet another 'very good proposal'. My once-in-a-life-time opportunity. They cannot come on Sunday but I am free for life," my sarcasm was in full form.

My mother played the shot she was best at. She started crying and left the room. I was the one who suffered and I hated people showing pity on me. On the other hand, my mother loved playing her victim card all the time. Sunny, who was standing at the door witnessing all this drama, gave me a 'just-play-along' look.

"But why does she want me to take a leave? I will come early in the evening," I asked him.

"She wants you to stay at home so that you can get ready properly."

This revelation of my mother's plan irked me even more.

The special guests finally arrived. Though I made no extra efforts other than the usual, I looked better today. I hate to admit it but she was right. Though it was not going to change much. I knew the fate of this evening.

I entered the living room without holding any tray. See, there are some benefits also of the artificial attachments. I wished everyone and caught the glimpse of the boy who was not bad, rather he was good. I thought he must be the brother or friend of the 'boy' as he was too good-looking for me.

"Come beta," my mother welcomed me in.

I took a quick glance while taking my seat. There was no other boy in the room. Only a middle-aged lady and he, were the visitors and of course my aunt who has come to this earth to rescue me of my miseries.

"Where are you working beta?" The lady asked me.

"KT Infotech, Gurgaon."

"That must be a good company. As a ...?"

"Aunty, I am Lead Manager."

"Ah..she joined some other post and was recently promoted within six months of joining. My daughter is very talented," my mother joined in.

I never knew she found me talented and did she forget that I joined as associate manager, when she mentioned 'some other post'?

"Yes of course, I told you na she got selected in ..." my aunt started to boast. I gave her a look which made her pause but couldn't stop her. "...Air Force" she completed with an ear-to-ear smile, moving her gaze from me to that lady.

Everyone in the room faked a broad smile at each other.

"Beta, why don't you two go and talk amongst yourself," the lady suggested looking at my father as if asking for his approval.

"Of course!" My mother added without waiting for my father's response. She had this unsaid privilege of acting on his behalf at her ease. "Beta take Aneesh ji to the t..terr..ace... Show him your balcony." Mom was quick to realise her mistake.

Aneesh, I liked the name. We sat in the balcony and he came carrying his cup of tea.

I liked his candidness. He seemed even better now or it was me taking a better look of him. He had a cute face and was fair-complexioned. I wondered why is he even considering me. This was my farthest point of progress so far. All my previous prospects did not even consider me for such casual chit-chat. However, I was not very hopeful. I knew at last, he too was going to say no, so why should I keep my curiosity to myself.

“Why are you here?”

“W...What ?” He was not expecting such a blunt question.

“I mean, why have you come to see me? You can find a much better girl than me.”

“So can you, but even you are here.”

I was confused. Was he blind or insane? “I ... I still don’t understand, why would you...”

“Accidents happen Bhavya. It can happen to anyone. It can happen with me too, before or after marriage. It’s not in our hands. What matters is, how we hold our life and how we move on, after life throws a challenge before us. How we muster the courage to face the world." His words felt like a cool breeze to me. "I was told you were selected in Indian Air Force. I am so proud of you and I am not sure if I even deserve you but I want to spend my life with a fighter like you. I like you," he emphasized his last three words or it could be my imagination.

I could not believe that someone, a rather good-looking one, was talking to me like this. Was this some kind of a joke? Was this a 'bakra thing' that Sunny watches on TV, where they put you in an awkward situation, record you and then make fun of you, in front of you? I actually started looking for that hidden camera around him.

"Won't you ask anything about me?"

"Let me absorb all this first," my thoughts abruptly came out.

He laughed and I joined him too. Nobody ever made me feel like this, even before the accident.

Everyone in the family was elated but my

mother was on the seventh sky as if I had hit a jackpot. The date of my marriage was soon decided and she started calling all our relatives to proudly announce it. I don't think even my selection of IAF matched anywhere with her this state of mind.

Life took a beautiful turn. The long phone calls, the dinners, the movies. Aneesh treated me so well and I never felt that I am any less than him.

Me and perhaps my parents too were skeptical the whole time, that something bad might happen at the last moment but finally, the day arrived.

I got married and he made me the queen of his life.

His relatives made some remarks though, to make me feel the magnitude of his sacrifice he had made by marrying me but I didn't care because he never made me feel that way.

A week after we came back from our honeymoon, I thought about my job. The reason I joined it was to escape the chaos of my home back then. Now I was ready to be a homemaker, taking care of him and his mother.

I was waiting for the right moment to discuss it with him. One afternoon, I found Aneesh sitting quietly lost in some thoughts.

"Hey, are you OK?" I asked, trying to sit.

"Yeah..," he said, and offered his hand to help. This was the only thing I didn't like him doing. It might take me some time but I wanted to do my chores on my own without any help.

"Doesn't seem so. Tell me what's the matter?"

"Nothing Bhavya, I am fine," he persisted.

"C'mon, please tell me," I could clearly make out with his tone that something was wrong.

He finally replied, "I lost my job. My company is closed."

"Oh, that's bad."

"But don't worry. I will sort this out."

"Of course, we will sort this out." This was no time to talk about leaving my job. I decided to join back my office for now, till things get stable.

Two months had passed and he was still jobless. I had been now taking care of all the household expenses, being the only one working. I could see how bad Aneesh felt about it.

One day Aneesh came home smiling. It was rare to find him in good mood these days.

"Hmm.. do you have something to share?" I tried to guess the answer.

He smiled back. "Bhavya, I got a job, but I am not sure if I can join."

"Wow, that's great, but why can't you join?"

"Not just that it's too far, maybe around two hours' drive from home, but it's timings are also odd. It's late evening to early morning shifts and ... even the salary is not much," he was disappointed.

"Oh, but I would suggest you join it and simultaneously you can look for better options."

"Yes, you are not wrong as the longer I sit back jobless the more difficult it would be to get one but if I join it, I wouldn't be able to spend time with you."

He was right but being jobless was affecting his mental state. He had started keeping aloof from me. "That's ok. It's a temporary phase. Don't think much and go for it."

Aneesh joined soon after and as expected, we hardly met now. He would return back at early morning hours and when he would be home, I had to go. He started sleeping in the other room as he didn't want to disturb me when he came back from work. His new job was very demanding and sometimes he had to go even on weekends.

It was one Saturday night and I woke up and saw him sitting in the balcony. It was midnight. I went to him.

"Oh, did I disturb you?" He asked, noticing me.

"It's you who seems disturbed. What happened?"

"I am fine. Was not feeling sleepy," he said. I didn't like his hiding things from me.

"Aneesh, tell me. I can see it on your face."

"Bhavya, my childhood friend Raunak is dying. He has cancer. He worked with me in my previous office and is jobless now. All his savings have already been drained. He has no money left for his treatment. I wish I could help him but ..."

"Hmm. Cancer needs costly treatment."

"Yes, but I can't see him dying. I wish I had money to help him."

"Don't worry Aneesh. We will do something."

I was proud of him for having such a kind and compassionate heart. I applied for a loan at my office.

Time went by and soon we were going to have our first anniversary. Aneesh was excited about it and wanted to have a gala evening, though I liked to keep it small and simple. I missed spending time with him, our quiet candle-lit dinners. Our financial condition was another reason I wanted to avoid the fancy celebration.

He requested me to book a five-star hotel for the party. I tried explaining him but he was not ready to change his mind. My credit card had already reached its limit and after the EMI deduction of the loan, it was getting difficult to manage. Aneesh's salary hardly contributed to the monthly expenses.

"Please do it one last time. I will repay all your money next month," he said. He didn't understand. It was not about repaying me. I was already over-stretched.

I was sitting at my office desk the next day, trying to think of a way to manage some extra bucks.

I received a call from Sunny.

"Didi, are you at the office?" He asked.

“Hi Sunny, How are you? Yes, I am at my office.”

“I am good. Didi are you free today evening?”

“Yes, I am. Are you planning to come home? Most wel...”

He interrupted me, “No, not at your home. I will see you at your office. I want to take you somewhere.”

“Where?” I was surprised.

“6.30 would be fine? I will come then. Please don’t tell anyone at your home about this. Just tell them you got stuck at the office,” I was curious to know what he was up to and why he wanted to keep it a secret.

“But why should I lie?”

“Please trust me. Just do what I say,” he hung up the phone abruptly.

What could be the matter and why does he want me to lie? I kept thinking about it.

He was waiting in Dad’s car at my office gate.

The same car Dad wanted to dispose of for so long. I thought he must have done it till now.

“Where are we going?” I asked Sunny.

“Just come Didi.” He bought some sandwiches on the way and handed me one. He still remembered my favourite Subway sandwiches. I grabbed a bite while still wondering where were we going.

After driving for almost an hour, we reached DLF Phase 1. I was trying to figure out why Sunny has brought me to this place. This was Gurgaon's one of the notorious place known for its indecent nightlife.

“Why have we come here?” I asked him.

“Wait Didi. Just keep sitting.”

“What’s the matter Sunny? Why are we waiting inside the car and for whom?” He started looking outside the window as if trying to avoid facing me. “Sunny, enough. Tell me clearly.”

“Aneesh came home yesterday, once again to ask for money.”

“For money..? Once again..? What do you mean?”

“Since your marriage, he has been coming on some pretext or the other and taking money from Dad. Two months back he took money for some treatment of his friend.”

I was shocked.

“Raunak?”

“Yes, that’s the name he told and this time he came for a lavish anniversary celebration that, as per him, you want to have.”

“I want to have? Sunny, in fact I..”

“I know Didi, I know you. I know he is lying this time too, as always.”

I did not want to believe what he said. “See, Sunny. Don’t take me wrong. I trust you completely and I know you are not lying but sometimes we misunderstand things.”

“Didi, I knew you won’t believe me, that's why I brought you here. Can you call him and ask where is he now?”

“Why do I need to do that? I know he is in his

office."

"Please Didi, just for once. Call him and ask."

Despite knowing this being a futile thing to do, I agreed and dialled his number.

"Hi Aneesh, Where are you?.. Of course... yaa I would be late... I had informed her...OK see you then.." The conversation ended and I confidently put my phone on the dashboard. "See I told you, he is at his office."

"And how far is his office from this place?"

"His office is in Noida, you know that," I was getting irritated now. "Why are you interrogating me like this?"

He noticed someone coming, "See for yourself Didi."

Some men were crossing the road and they went inside the bar. I saw a known face amongst them. It had turned dark by now, so it took me some time to recognise him. It was Aneesh.

"Is he?"

"Yes, it's him."

I read the signboard of the place he entered – The Fun Night Strip Club.

"But he said he was at his office."

"He is not going to any office. This is his regular adda. I have been keeping an eye on him. He comes here almost daily. He was not working anywhere even before marriage. He was in huge debt that he repaid with the money Dad gave him," Sunny revealed everything in a go.

I was stunned.

"Dad gave him money too? I was only aware of the car and the gold items he gave to him and his mother. Do you know how much?"

"I don't know what exactly he gave in marriage but till now Dad has given him around twenty five lakhs. I overheard him talking to Mom."

"Why did they need to do this? Were they aware of all this before marriage?"

"I don't know how much they already knew

but when I told them they didn't seem that surprised. Rather Mom asked me not to tell you. You know how she is."

The way Mom reacted did not come as a surprise to me. I had seen how desperately she wanted to get me married. But I always trusted Dad, that if required, he would take a stand for me and would not blindly follow her. Why did he feel the need to give him that money? Just because he married me? Why did he feel the need to pay this compensation all through his life?

I felt so low about myself. I never knew I was such a big burden for them.

"Oh Gosh. He has been robbing us right on our face and we could not see. Soon after marriage I have been running the house. I have been making all expenses, big or small. I gave him money too for Raunak's treatment," I confessed.

Sunny placed his hand over my shoulder, "He lied about Raunak too. He was that guy in the leather jacket with him."

I could not speak any further.

"Didi, you come home with me. I wanted to show you all this so that I can take you home with me."

"Did Mom or Dad ask you to… ?"

His voice was choked now. "Mom thinks everything will get fine with time and after marriage, that's your house now and you should learn to adjust there. But I don't agree with her. You have been cheated and you have all the right to come back to your home."

"Thanks, Sunny. I wish every sister gets a brother like you so that girls are not treated as a burden. I lost my leg but not my strength. I am still earning not only for myself but for those two parasites also. I can very well manage myself."

"I know and I am proud of you," Sunny was in tears.

"Thanks, I wish Mom and Dad too had that trust in me. Anyways," I moved to get out of the car.

"Where are you going?" he asked.

"He needs to confront me, confront his wife."

"It's not a good place. Please don't go inside."

"I need to do this for myself. Just wait for me."

I went inside the dimly lit area. I looked around and he could easily be found, enjoying his time, ogling a pole dancer and making obscene gestures towards her. I could not believe this disgusting person right in front of me, was the same man I married and I loved blindly. I went straight to him.

"Bh.. Bh... Bhavya, what are you doing here?"

I put a tight slap on his face. He and his friends were dumbstruck.

I came outside. Sunny was standing near the gate.

"Can you drop me home?" I asked him.

"Didi, you can come to your own home with me, I will handle it. You don't need to go to

Aneesh's house."

"I need to, Sunny. I need to settle this once and for all and don't worry I am strong enough to handle this.

I came back home and was awake since early morning hours. I heard Aneesh coming at 3.30 am but he did not come to me.

At least he had that much shame left in him, at least I thought so. I decided to let him sleep peacefully one last time.

I got up early, packed up my stuff and was sipping my cup of tea when my mother-in-law woke up.

"What the matter *bahu*? What's this drama?" She was pointing to my bags.

"The drama?" I smiled. "Maa ji, rather it's the end of the drama now. Could you please wake up Aneesh, before I leave? We need to talk.

"Aneesh .. see what your wife is up to. Aneeeeesh...," she repeated when she got no response from him.

He came out rubbing his eyes.

“What’s the matter? Why are you making so much noise?

“Your beloved wife is leaving,” she said.

“What nonsense? Have you gone mad?” Aneesh said to me.

“No, I am back to my senses.”

“Just because I spared you last night and did not hit you back, you think you are some *Jhansi ki Rani*, who can do anything she wants to.”

“You spared me last night?” I was astonished at his shamelessness.

“What, you hit my son? You bitch!” My mother-in-law reacted.

“Maa ji, mind your language!” I spoke loud and clear.

She was not expecting my retaliation. “You are such a mean and selfish girl. My son ruined his life for you and this is what you are doing in return? What do you think of yourself? Did you know he got so many proposals, still he married you, an ugly handicapped girl."

"Whatever I am and whatever I was, I never hid my reality. I never lied. But your son, he is a complete lie. Are you aware where is he going? With whom is he spending his nights? What job is he doing?" My anger raised the pitch of my voice.

"I know and what else should he do? He is young and handsome. What's the harm? After all, you are one he is married to and not those girls. You are having the privilege of being called the daughter-in-law of this house."

"I don't believe this. You people are disgusting even beyond my imagination," I turned to Aneesh. "And you Aneesh, what have you to say? Was begging before your wife not enough that you went to my Dad to beg?"

"How dare you? It was your family who came begging to us to marry you not me and I am a man, your husband. I can do anything and I have full right to your money. And about your father? He is a cheat. He had promised us forty lakhs in marriage and gave only twenty. I go there to have the rest of my money. I did not force them to pay. It was their decision. If they did not have the money, why did they come to me?" The hidden demon inside him came out.

"Thanks Aneesh, for letting me know your true colours. I can't stay here for one more moment."

"Go. Go right now but remember one thing, once you leave you can never come back again. I can easily get a new wife then don't come back crying to me."

"Mr. Aneesh, when I can get my dead limb removed from my body and can earn a dignified life for myself, I don't have to bear a sick relation like you to survive. Though you might need another woman to earn for you. So, I have one piece of advice. Next time when you go to ruin some other life, please make sure to tie your rate card around your neck," I was burning with anger. "I give you ten days of time for returning all the money you took from me and from my Dad and all the stuff you got from us in the name of dowry. If you fail to return by that time, be ready to face legal action," they were blown away by my words, "and yes, don't worry. I spare the monthly expenses I bore for you both. Keep it as my rent payment for using your house."

Leaving both of them stunned, I came outside. I had already googled the location of the nearest hotel and was waiting for the cab.

A car parked at a distance drove closer to me. It was Sunny. I couldn't hold my tears back when I saw Dad sitting with him and Mom too in the back seat.

Dad came out and patted my head, "We were waiting for you. Come, let's go home."

I opened the back door to find Mom crying. "I am sorry beta." She said and hugged me.

Bhavya was still standing in front of me.

I felt like standing up and giving her a big salute. She could not join the Force, but she indeed is a soldier.

"I am speechless. What a warrior! Sometimes in order to protect our children, we end up making their lives even more difficult, but as a fighter she fought it through," I said.

"Yes, this label of being married and settled seems so important to us that we fall prey to vultures like Aneesh," the compartment remarked.

"Proud of this woman, who was strong enough to prove the people wrong. Her bodily defect is no reason for her to tolerate such a mess."

"Indeed."

A child entered playfully swinging her head. Another lady with her, most probably her mother, held her hand and they took their seats. She was singing a rhyme to her.

The girl's curiosity immediately made her jump back to face the window.

"She is so cute."

"Who? Riya or her mother Ramaa?"

"You can't start without me. That's not fair."

"Hahaha, OK. Come."

.

"Falling down does not make you a failure.

Not getting up makes you one."

RAMAA

He loved travelling. He believed in living in the present and took every opportunity to steal some time from his routine and sneak into a vacation. Akash, my husband, worked as a chief executive in an automobile company. Despite his busy schedule he knew how to balance work and family. He never made either me or Riya feel neglected.

We had come back from Nainital that night, after the weekend break, our last trip together.

"Ah, I always enjoy being in the hills. It was a lovely time. Isn't it?" Akash said, closing his diary and handing it over to me.

I mentally ticked off all my 'before sleep to-do items' and kept his diary in the cupboard. "Yes, Riya loved it," I said, adjusting my pillow.

"What about you? How do you like it?"

"Of course, I enjoyed it too," I said, popping my pill.

"Ramaa, What's about that pill? I saw you taking one in the morning too. Not well?"

"Ah, my usual migraine. I will be fine by morning," I said, switching off the lights.

"Oh, you know what, I wanted to tell..."

"Mmm...Let's sleep. Tell me tomorrow. I am so tired now." I said with a half-asleep voice.

I wish I had let him complete what he wanted to say. Had I known that was my last night with him, those were his last words to me.

The next morning came with lifelong darkness for me. I didn't notice him when I woke up but when I came to him with his bed-tea, I found his eyes wide open and hands dropped off.

“Akaaaasshh!” I screamed.

The hopeless faces of the doctors and nurses made me even more nervous. My neighbours were speaking to them but I could not make any sense of what was happening around me.

“Bhabhi, come sit here,” one of our neighbours said to me.

“When can I See Akash?”

“Bhabhi, have this glass of water.”

“Tell the doctors to hurry up. We need to leave soon. I looked towards the door of his ICU room. “Akash, get up, we need to go. Riya is waiting for us at home.”

Then I felt a known hand on my shoulder. I turned back. It was Maa.

“Maa, Maa, see…He is not listening to me. Maa tell him na,” she was just crying and not responding to me. I turned to my neighbours again, "Bhaiya please tell them to wake him up."

I was screaming and crying. Maa hugged me. She too was crying uncontrollably when she uttered, "He is gone. He is gone forever."

It was not only Akash, who died. My life died too. My existence died too.

Cardiac arrest, I could not believe it. He was perfectly fine. He was there with me a few hours back. How could he die? How could I not save him? How could I be sleeping unknowingly when he left? Had I not taken that pill that day. Maybe he had tried to wake me up. The questions kept burning inside me.

I had no idea what happened for the next few days. I was doing the rituals as told. Friends, relatives and neighbours came and consoled me. Some ladies hugged me and cried but I could not feel a thing. All I felt was a deep void, a deep pain inside me. I wanted to end my life but I had to survive for Riya.

She was just a toddler and too young to even understand what had happened.

I had completely lost it when Rajat, Akash's brother, handled the things. He took care of everything around.

He lived in Meerut and managed a grocery shop there. Akash had once shared that at a very young age, Rajat fell prey to the wrong company and became a drug addict. He left his home and went to Meerut. The family also broke all ties with him but their mother could not bear this and died soon after.

I first met him at the time of the death of my father-in-law. It was only then that he came to know about his mother too. He was guilty of his acts and held himself responsible for their parent's death.

Akash was in regular touch with him, since then. He bought him the shop at Meerut so that he could earn his living as he had hardly any means to manage.

Today Rajat stood strong and was managing everything, all the paperwork and all other stuff with Akash's company, as I had no idea of it at all. Akash always used to tell me about them but I never cared to listen. I never wanted to know about them, when he was there to manage it all. Never had I, in my wildest dreams, thought of this moment.

One day I found Rajat discussing something with my mother with a pile of papers in his hand.

“I know Aunty, she is not in the right state of mind to do this, but she has to decide soon as they give a limited time to submit the application.”

Akash’s company had the policy of offering compensatory employment in the event of the death of their employee. Rajat was right. I was not ready for this and I was never going to be. How could I take his place in his office? I didn’t have the courage to see that place, that building, that seat that he occupied. But I had to think of Riya, so I decided to apply for it.

After around three months, I joined the office, Akash’s office. I neither had earlier ever thought of working nor did I feel any need for it. Being a simple, small town girl, I was happy being the homemaker. Akash encouraged me initially to enroll for some professional course and pursue a career. He believed that women should be financially independent but I was never interested and when Riya came into our lives, there was no question about it.

I was pondering sitting in my office whether Akash was watching me at the moment. He must be happy that I am independent now, as he had wanted. It was indeed a very costly independence.

Though he was gone, I felt him close to me with each passing breath but I was not able to answer Riya's questions. She could not understand why and where had her Papa gone.

Rajat did his best to keep Riya engaged but I knew she was waiting for her father to come back.

It's said, time is the best healer. But I feel it

doesn't heal, time makes you learn to live with your wound for life.

A week had passed since Akash's *barsi*. It was a different Sunday morning when I saw my mother smiling after long. She was sitting on the terrace reading something on her phone.

"What's it, Maa?" I asked, watering the plants.

"Sanjay got his posting here, in Delhi. He will be shifting soon," she said, putting her phone down. "It's been almost four years since I last saw him," she said, taking a deep breath. She seemed to have lost in her fond memories with her brother.

Sanjay Uncle, being a police inspector, got his transfers frequently and Maa could not catch up with him for long. It would be nice for her to meet him.

"Ramaa beta, I need to talk," her tone signalled she had something on her mind.

She had been staying with me most of the time since then. She might now want to spend some time with her brother. I could understand and was anyways looking for daycare options for Riya.

“Yes Maa, tell me,” I sat on the chair next to her.

“Beta, I can understand your situation, your pain. It has been seven years since your Dad left us and I am not yet able to come at par with it.”

“Yes Maa, I miss him too, but now I feel more deeply what you must have gone through.”

“Don’t take me wrong but your situation is different, beta. When your Dad left me, you were grown up and I had lived my almost entire life with him but you have your whole life in front of you, and look at Riya.”

“What do you mean, Maa? Please say it clearly.”

“You need to re-settle. You should think of a second marriage.”

“Maa, what are you saying?” I got up from my chair. How could she even think of this? “I am settled. I don’t need anyone in my life. I will take care of Riya too and who says I am alone. Akash is always with me."

"Beta, be practical. A young girl cannot survive alone. You might not need a husband but Riya needs a father."

"Enough Maa. Please don't ever bring up this topic again."

"Beta, try to..."

"Mumma, would you pack my lunch please. Pack me a cheese sandwich." Riya's cute plea interrupted Maa and I was glad she did.

"Pack for what beta? Where are you going?" I bent over my knees to her.

"Oh Mumma, you always forget. Today is Sundayyy. Rajat Uncle is coming. We are going to see Avenge...rs.." She said and the way she was stretching her words showed all her excitement."

Rajat had been taking extra care of her since then. Either he would come over to play with her or took her out almost every weekend. Last weekend, they went to the Rail Museum and she enjoyed there a lot. She was chatting about it that whole night.

I was glad that Riya came just on time to save me from that conversation. I went inside to pack her bag.

But you know mothers. No matter how much you keep on saying, they would never leave their persistence for what they had decided.

Exactly after one week, the next Sunday afternoon I was filling up Riya's school admission form and my fingers froze at the column of father's name. Maa, who was sitting next to me, came up with it again. She perhaps saw my tears.

"Beta, you need that relationship for your life, Riya's life."

"Maa, please. I told you already," I was fed up now convincing her, "Do you think anyone else would be able to give that love and affection to Riya?

"Rajat would be," she instantaneously said.

"What? Rajat? How could I marry him? And why would he marry me?" I understood his sympathies with Riya but why would somebody take this liability for the whole of his life. "Wait, how did this name occur to you? I hope you did not talk to him about this?"

"He, himself proposed."

"What? Rajat proposed to marry me?" I was still trying to believe what she said when the doorbell rang.

It was him. He had come to pick up Riya and it was now too embarrassing to face him. Maa exchanged some looks with him as if to convey that I have been told, and left the living room. He came over and sat near me. I was trying to get up.

"Ramaa, please sit," he said.

"Rajat, I need ... to..."

"Calm down and just sit," he probably read my dilemma.

I sat down with a sigh.

"Ramaa, I understand the emotional turmoil you are going through. Akash was a very joyful and kind person. He was my buddy more than my brother. He accepted me wholeheartedly after all that I did to my family."

The mention of Akash made me feel better sitting there. My eyes were wet again. These tears had always been in my eyes since that night. They just needed a small prompt and they would come out flooding.

"He has done many favours to me. I had no money, no job, nothing. I was finished but he gave me a new life. He helped me set up my shop so that I could live with dignity. Whatever I am today, it's all because of him. I would always be indebted to him."

"So, you thought of repaying him by helping me, by marrying me?"

"No, please don't think that way. I could never repay him and you don't need any help. Akash was always full of praises for you, how nicely you manage your home and Riya and now I see that. He wanted to give all happiness to you and Riya. Now I want to give, what he could not do."

"Rajat, I don't know how to react to this. I am

grateful for what you are doing for us, especially Riya but I cannot marry. I cannot give Akash's place to you or to anyone."

Riya again came from her room at the right moment with her little bag and gave him a tight hug. "Uncle, I am ready. I have packed my doll, my clay dough and my unicorn. Let's gooo," her eyes sparkled in excitement.

He smiled at her, "Okay, let's goooo," imitating her cute tone.

He held her hand and was about to leave when he looked back at me, "Let me fill her void at least if I cannot do yours."

I was perturbed. I knew I could manage alone but what about Riya? Would she be able to manage too? Was I being unfair to her? Was Maa right?

Life is unpredictable. I never thought I would be taking Akash's place in his office and I never ever thought I would even consider giving Akash's place in my life to anyone else.

Rajat was trying every bit to be for Riya and for me too.

That day, it was Riya's interaction at school for her admission. I wanted to go there alone with Riya but she was too adamant. "Mumma, please let Uncle also come. Without him, I would forget my poems," she said.

Rajat took her in his lap. "No, you would not. You know them by heart and we revised it thoroughly. Now listen to your Mumma."

He made her prepare her poems for school. I felt Riya would feel good if he comes along.

"It's OK. You can join, if you wish."

"Of course, I would love to."

It was too awkward to go with Rajat and sit on those two seats in the school with Riya, meant for the child's parents. I felt as if I was cheating on Akash. Why was God putting me through all this?

Riya did well and while we were coming back, I realized I had to go to the bank.

"Could you just drop me here? I had some work at the bank."

"What is it?" He asked. He was usually taking care of all such things.

"Need to give one application and need to withdraw some money."

"You can give me that application and the cheque. Tomorrow it's your office. Just relax with Riya and give me all the papers. I will do it after I drop you both home."

Why was he doing this? Why was he protecting me, when I already told him I cannot... I needed to stop this.

"It's OK. I'll do it some other day."

There was a constant conflict going on inside me and Maa also left no chance.

"Don't make him wait for long. He can marry any girl but you won't get anyone else like Rajat who cares so much for you and Riya."

Her words, Rajat's affection for Riya, and Riya's twinkling eyes, all these were making me go crazy.

I could not sleep that night. I saw Akash's

photo kept on the bedside. I was trying to search for the answers in his smile. I tried to recall what he used to do when he had to decide on something and his diary occurred to me. He used to write. I got up and looked for it in the cupboard where I last kept it that night. I picked it up and could feel the warmth of his hands. I opened the pages and touched those words. My tears were dripping on the pages. Then I noticed something, some details. It was his policy details. 'SKC Term Insurance.. 2 cr, KLB Life Insurance.. 40 lakhs' and there were other deposit details. I was afraid these might have been lapsed and thought of asking Rajat to check. It was him only, who took care of all these things. But when I say I can manage alone, then why should I ask Rajat or anyone else to check?

I opened my laptop and entered the policy details. I was surprised to see that they have been paid up to my account. I could not recall filling up the forms of any of these insurance companies.

I checked my account to see the details. I was astonished to see the amount was credited in June itself. The very next month of Akash's death and what I saw next was even more shocking.

I thoroughly read every page of the diary. I had enough to keep me awake the whole night.

Maa knocked at my door the next morning.

"Awake already?"

"Yes Maa, I am wide awake now," I said and picked up my phone to call Rajat but he had already dropped me a message.

'Hi, Good Morning. How's Riya? Get ready with that application. I will drop you at your office on the way.'

'See you at 3.' I replied.

Maa came over to my room again, "What are you busy with since morning. Not going to the office today?"

"Yes, Maa. Just needed to wind up a few things.," I smiled back at her, taking my eyes off my screen.

I made a few phone calls and picked up my bag to leave.

"Where are you going?" Maa asked.

"I am just coming Maa. I will be back in an hour," I said.

It took me more time though. Maa was waiting for me at lunch.

I received his message again. 'I'm on my way. About to reach.' The doorbell rang twenty minutes later.

"Hi, come in. Maa, see who has come."

He raised an eyebrow at my unusual comment. Even Maa gave me a puzzled look wiping her hands with the kitchen towel. It was no surprise as he was a regular visitor.

"What happened? You didn't go to the office today? You seem tired," he asked with concern.

"Yaa, I was not feeling good."

"So many times, I tell you not to overexert yourself. You need to take care of yourself," he said.

“But where does she listen? Since morning she has been busy with those files and all,” Maa said.

“Why didn’t you tell me? Let me help you. What is it?” he asked.

I smiled and took a deep breath.

“Yes, why do I need to do this, when you are there,” I said and gave him a piece of paper. “You wanted the application. Here, take it. Please go through this.”

Rajat read the paper and looked up at me. All that concern and care vanished from his face. I could literally see his cunning mask getting off.

“I had already sent it to the bank and to the police station too. This is for your information.”

Maa got anxious. “What? Police? What’s going on? Ramaa tell me, what happened?”

“Mr. Rajat Arora, are you going to tell your prospective mother-in-law, or should I disclose?”

"I am leaving," his sugar-coated tone was gone now.

"No, you cannot. You need to answer. How much did you owe to Akash?"

The bell rang again.

"Maa, can you please?" I said pointing to the door, "It must be Sanjay Uncle."

"Sanjay? Why would he...?" She went to the door when it rang again and was surprised to find my guess correct. "Would anyone tell me what is happening?" Maa was distressed now.

Sanjay Uncle came in uniform with a constable with him.

"Let me tell you Maa. Akash had taken a loan of forty lakhs from his office for this cheat. He bluffed him. He never gave up drugs and is still an addict. Akash not only bought him the shop but a house too and this cheat, he lost it all to his lenders," I held my tears back. "But that's not all, Akash's death gave him another plan to rob us. He took advantage of my trust and took my signatures, and stole all the policy benefits. He also forged my signatures and got the phone number changed in my account so that I do not receive any alert message from the bank." He was standing shamelessly. "Now I understand why you were being so protective."

"Rajat, is this all true?" Maa looked at Rajat.

"Maa, you still want to trust him? See this."

I handed her a paper, my account statement, that had multiple withdrawals running into lakhs with remarks- 'Cheque paid in favour of Rajat Arora'.

"Oh my God. But how did he get you to sign those cheques?"

"I never signed them, Maa. He did not leave the chance to encash his own brother's death and look at his guts! He wanted to dwell on it all his life and planned to marry me," my eyes were fuming with anger.

"What did you say that day Mr. Rajat , 'I am indebted to him.' Yes, you are and now I will make sure you repay for the whole of your life."

"OK. I did it but I was taking care of you and Riya too. Did you forget that?" He shamelessly blurted.

"And who asked you to do it?" I screamed at him.

"If not me, somebody else would take advantage of you. You should be thankful. I was at least marrying you. Else, why would I marry a widow that too with a child," there was not even a pinch of guilt in his words.

"Get Lost!" I turned away, "Uncle please take him away from my eyes, else I will kill him."

"Come Mr. Fraud, and be thankful to her that she did not marry you else you would have been charged under Section 494 also, for not disclosing your first marriage," uncle said watching the constable handcuffing him, "Ramaa, your doubts were correct. I checked with the Modipuram police station. He is already married and his wife left him being sick of his abuse."

"I am not surprised," I said, taking a deep

breath.

Uncle left with him. Maa slumped on the sofa still in shock, “What did I think of him and what was his cruel reality? He was cheating you right under my nose and yet I could not see it.”

“Maa, it’s our fault too. We are also responsible to some extent that people like Rajat cheat on us. Why do we women feel the need for a man to survive? Yes, I lost Akash and I am going to miss him all my life but I am fine and have accepted it. I want to live with his memories. He always said that women should be independent and he was so right. I would make sure Riya follows this and does not fall prey to another bastard like Rajat. I do not need any other relationship for me or Riya to strive. I am complete.”

“Yes, you are right beta. You are indeed complete.”

"Scoundrel. Cheating on his own dead brother and his family who trusted him, gave him another chance. But they rightly say, 'once a cheat always a cheat,'' I said with a frown.

"No, that's not fair to judge everyone for what Rajat did. Some people do change, but that's not important. Important is how we can allow these people to exploit us?" said the compartment.

"True. Ramaa was happy in her own li'l world but when tragedy struck her, she gathered herself well. It's the attitude of society making us feel helpless and incomplete that we fall prey to such pitfalls," I said.

"Getting into another relationship is not wrong, but just because you need a man in your life to survive is sheer foolishness," the compartment said.

"I am glad Ramaa was able to uncover the truth before it was too late."

"Yes, and by late I remember, you must be getting late for your office. You already missed your station, Mandi House, a few minutes back.

How could I forget, it can know my destination.

"Hahaha, you keep forgetting my talents."

"OK, I will get down at the next interchange."

"I understand. These stories are so mesmerizing it's hard to leave them."

"Yaa, one last time please before I get down at Kirti Nagar."

"Fine. Let me take you to Bhaumi. The one in blue

saree."

She was reading a book thoughtfully. I felt a 'no-nonsene' vibe in her.

"Do not wait for someone else to take a stand for you.

Take the lead. Do it for yourself."

BHAUMI

I failed to meet my own expectations. All I wanted was to nurture my sisters and to give them a stable life that destiny tried to snatch away. I wanted them to succeed in their lives but I failed miserably.

Pooja and Nisha, both grew up as arrogant and self-centred and cared for no one else. They only knew to receive and never learnt to give, be it love, care or respect.

Life was calm back then in my hometown, Sunder Nagar but everything changed after that night. It has been more than two decades now. We lost our father, serving his duty at the rescue mission in Uttarakhand.

He always used to say 'Duty Comes First' and he walked his talk.

I was twenty one then, just out of college. Maa went into a deep state of shock and started keeping unwell. I had no time to remorse as I had to become 'the man of the house'. I never liked the rat race of the corporate world and wanted to follow my passion of painting but was hardly left with any choice. I had to earn for the family. Pooja was fifteen and Nisha, twelve at that time.

I managed a decent job in Delhi and we shifted here. Just like me, my sisters too were missing the carefree life back in Sunder Nagar.

I started taking them out for city tours more often, to make them feel good about this place. India Gate soon became their favourite spot and *Bittu Tikki Wala,* their favourite eatery. I still remember their cute faces munching their favourite snacks.

Surviving in a metro city was never easy and with my new job I was hardly managing the household expenses and had to spend every penny thoughtfully but I loved spending it on them. I wanted to usher all happiness on them. After all, they were too young for all this.

I started looking for alternate income avenues and late evening tuitions came as a handy option and suited my schedule too.

Life changed with time and soon the girls became part of the city life. Pooja joined college and Nisha started preparing for Engineering entrance tests along with her senior secondary. I even managed to buy a flat of my own.

I was happy and content in my world but Vaibhav changed it all. He had recently joined our office and I first noticed him that day, when he came by my seat.

"Hi Bhaumi, I am new to this place. Can you suggest some good cafes or restaurants?" He was standing at my desk. I read his name from his I-Card and stared at him with a blank face. He read my 'Do-I-know-you' look.

"Hey! I am Vaibhav from the testing team. We had our intro during the last review meeting."

He sounded disappointed with my memory

skills. Being good-looking, he might not be used to such straight looks from girls. By now I recalled him being a hot topic of discussion among the other girls in our office. The 'charming Chandigarh guy', I heard them often gossiping in the cafeteria.

"Can you suggest a few?" He came back to his question.

I found it stupid to walk over to someone for a thing that you can easily google, but I had a soft corner for people moving out from their hometowns to these big cities for earning. It's so unfair. I dutifully gave him some suggestions.

"Oh..actually...I was wondering if you could ...a..accompany me, to any one of these? Your favourite one, of course," I finally caught the signal. He was asking me out.

"Some other day," I politely replied and went back to my computer screen.

"Can't you see stupid? He is interested in you! Why can't you let your guards off for once damn it?" Himakshi whispered, sliding her chair towards me.

Himakshi was more than a colleague. She

was one of the few with whom I could confide in.

“Have you completed your report? I am still behind my schedule.” I changed the topic and went back to my screen.

My life revolved around Maa, Pooja and Nisha, and had no time to think beyond it.

That was the last weekend of the month which I usually dedicated to calculating the monthly expenses, when Pooja came to me. I was always going over my budget with the addition of some new items every month. This time it was the EMI deduction for the loan I took for Nisha’s scooty.

“Di, I need to do some shopping for my college fest. Can you give me some money?” Pooja said.

“Hmm... I need to cut down on some of the expenses to get through this,” I was engrossed in my self-talk.

“Di, I need around five-six thousand,” Pooja spoke again, this time a bit louder and the figure caught my attention.

“Um...can this wait for some time?” I was mentally calculating Maa’s health check-up that was due next month. I had forgotten to add this earlier.

“It’s a college fest. It’s next week only!” Pooja emphasised ‘college’ as if I didn’t understand its meaning.

“OK...OK Let me figure it out,” though I had no idea how I was going to do it.

While I was still puzzled with my calculations, she left murmuring. She was getting aggressive every now and then and compared her lifestyle with her affluent college mates. I was trying to keep up as much as possible but was always short of her expectations.

The next morning, I handed over three thousand bucks to her.

“Could you manage with this for now?”

“What is this? Only three thousand?” Pooja was disappointed but she took the money.

“Hey Di, what about the money I asked for my new phone?” Nisha came by.

“Next month, I promise,” I said to Nisha.

“Every time you do this to me. You make me plead for every single penny,” Nisha complained and left, tossing her feet.

I turned back to leave but my feet froze when I heard Pooja saying something again, “Had Dad been alive today...”

It felt as if somebody had put a dagger right into my chest. Even I wanted to say, “Had my Dad been alive today.”

Maa understood my helplessness and she tried to save as much as possible by cutting down at her needs.

I know when she turned down the housemaid, it was not because of the quality of her work as she had remarked, it was to save that money.

I didn’t want her to exhaust herself as her health was more important. Moreover, it was Pooja and Nisha who needed to cut down the expenses but she opined that they were young and full of desires. They were justified in their demands. I had no other option than to abide by her.

It was lunchtime the other day, and I was at the terrace of my office, lost in my thoughts when a voice interrupted.

"Hi," Vaibhav uttered in excitement.

"Hello," my tone was cold enough to give him that 'Do not Disturb' signal.

"I never knew you could be found anywhere other than your desk," he either did not notice that signal or chose to ignore it.

I remained silent trying to drag myself out of my thoughts.

"So, how are you doing?" He probably found nothing better to break that embarrassing silence.

"Yaa, I am fine. Was feeling suffocated, so I thought of coming here," I said with a half-hearted smile and wondered why I felt the need to give him that explanation.

"Yes, indeed. Even I find staying in that four-by-four cubicle so depressing. We spend almost the entire day in such compact spaces. It's really suffocating."

"Not just the day in office. We spend our

entire lives in such self-imposed cubicles as if we are stuck in some maze and there is no way out," I didn't realise when I allowed those words to come out. How could I allow anyone to sense my pain?

"Bhaumi, if there is something bothering you, you can share with me," his tone turned serene.

I didn't like anyone intruding in my personal space. It's my life, my pain and my problems. Why should I share it with anyone else? But at the same time, I found his words soothing. I felt him genuinely willing in easing my pain but I could not allow this to happen.

Before I revealed any further, I smiled back and quickly changed the topic, "How did you like Delhi?"

"Oh yeah! I am simply loving the daily travel from Mayur Vihar to Patel Nagar and then spending the entire day at my desk and checking the reverse route to my flat. It's so thrilling !" he added sarcastically.

I could not stop myself from laughing and he joined me too. He was the second person after Himakshi, with whom I had laughed outside my family circle. She always used to say that my customary hellos are accompanied with smiles not an inch more than the required length.

"I heard there are a lot of good restaurants in C.P., I am gonna check them out on my birthday. But what's the fun of celebrating alone!" he tried once more, raising an eyebrow.

"When is your birthday?" I liked the way he asked. It was smarter than his last try.

"Tomorrow," he blurted.

This time I could not say no, "OK, I would come only on the condition that you are going to tell me your real birthday."

"Hmm... smart move. Let's talk about it tomorrow," he smiled at his lie being caught.

The first meeting led to another and so on. Finally, I ended up into something I always wanted to stay away from. With Vaibhav, I felt like part of some different world. It was such a beautiful feeling to be loved, to be taken care of. He made me feel special. I felt so lively with him but at the same time, I had this guilt inside me as if I was shirking my responsibilities. Himakshi was so excited when she came to know about Vaibhav and me.

"I am so happy for you. You two look so good together," she said.

"Stop Himakshi. You are taking it too far. I am already scared."

"Scared of what?"

"I need to tell him that I cannot commit anything."

"What is that supposed to mean? Are you not happy with him?"

"Of course, I am. I love him and want to settle down with him but you know I can't."

"No, I don't know. Please explain, why can't you?"

"How can I leave my family and think about myself? How can I be so mean?"

"Have you gone out of your mind? It's not you who is being mean. Rather it's your family."

"Himakshi! Stop right there."

"No, I won't. Why can't you face the truth? You are always thinking of your sisters but all they want is your money. They give a damn to you and your life. I understand that after the loss of the family's breadwinner, the eldest child has to take the responsibility of filling the void. But what about others? Who gave them the right to play victim all the time? Have they ever thought about you? Look at you. You are already thirty. Has anyone thought about your marriage? I am surprised even Aunty...?"

No, it's not like that. I already told her that I am not interested in marriage."

"And she agreed? I hate to say this but she is aware that they cannot survive without you, so she is happy with your sacrifice. And If you are thinking, you are doing any good to your sisters, you are grossly mistaken. They take you for granted. You have actually spoiled them by meeting all their legitimate and illegitimate demands."

"Himakshi, please. You are taking them all wrong. Who else will they look upto, if not me?"

"My dear, it's not who else, the question is

till when? OK, Tell me one thing. You are working overtime, and have been taking tuitions also to earn an extra few bucks to manage your house. What are they doing to contribute? Only cribbing?"

Her questions were sharp and straight and I had no answers to it.

"Bhaumi, it's high time you start thinking about yourself. It's not being selfish, it's being sane. Life rarely gives a second chance. You cannot afford to miss it."

I was in a deep dilemma when I came back home that evening. Maa cheerfully opened the door. I could not recall when I last saw her that happy. Nisha had cleared her entrance test and she proudly showed me her call letter. All I could see was 'Admission Amount : Rs 10.50 lakhs'. I recalled my Dad's mantra – 'Duty Comes First' and it cleared all my doubts.

I texted Vaibhav to meet.

"Hi, it's my lucky day today. It's the first time you called to see me," Vaibhav was in his usual peppy mood.

I could not look into his eyes. "We need to talk."

"And I am all ears," he replied with his charming smile.

"Vaibhav, I...I am sorry...I cannot continue in this relationship," I said, crushing the edge of my dupatta.

He paused for a moment. "What... What happened?"

"I already told you everything about my family. I am not ready yet."

"Fine. I am not asking you to marry me right now. I am in no hurry. Honestly speaking I am, but it's OK. I can wait."

"You don't understand, Vaibhav. I don't know when I can get married. I don't see myself in any relationship in the near future."

"What do you mean?"

"I mean, how can I? Pooja is not settled yet and Nisha has just got her admission and needs to leave for the hostel. Maa is also not keeping well. How can I even think about myself, leaving all this behind?"

"Bhaumi, where am I on your list? These things, these liabilities of your life, would never end and I am not asking you to leave anything. I already said, we will do everything possible to support your family. I respect your decision and I am proud of you but that doesn't mean you need to be stuck like this endlessly," he was not ready to listen.

"Well, let me make this clear. Until both my sisters are settled well, I won't even think of marriage." I had to put it straight.

Vaibhav pushed his chair away and asked with an intense look, "So, where does it take us?"

I was unable to have the courage to answer him but could not let him suffer with me anymore, "I don't know... You can move on."

"Really!! Is this what you have for me at the end of the day?" Vaibhav banged his fist on the table and left.

I wanted to stop him. I wanted to be with him. I wanted to marry him. But I knew I could not.

Himakshi was enraged when Vaibhav told her about my decision.

“I don't believe this. He is head over heels for you. You are putting your love, your life, your everything at stake for your thankless sisters.”

“Himakshi, why don’t you understand?"

“It’s not me, dear. It’s you who need to understand and if you are adamant to ruin your life, go ahead but mark my words you are going to repent it. You are going to miss him all your life.”

She was absolutely right.

Life moved on and soon Nisha completed her degree and Pooja also got married to his college friend, Raman. I was happy that things were turning stable and the decision I took about my life was worth it.

Raman was a mature and understanding guy. Though Pooja was arrogant and demanding, I hoped after marriage she would change. But that’s what I had been hoping for since her adolescence. Unfortunately, she proved me wrong again.

Within a year, she had come back home thrice fighting over some petty arguments with Raman or his parents. Me and Maa kept counselling her again and again but her tantrums kept increasing and now Nisha too had started following in her footsteps.

It was yet another day when she had come back sulking over the choice of Raman's new car. As always, we were trying to counsel her, but that day she said something unbearable.

"Think calmly, Pooja. Marriage, like all relationships, needs time," I said to her.

"Please. At least you don't preach about marriage. You hardly know about it. It's not easy to stay in your in-laws house. You don't know the pressure on us married girls."

"Us married girls?" I repeated her last words to myself that alienated me.

"Beta, girls need to adjust in marriage," Maa said, almost pleading to her. I was surprised how she ignored the taunting remarks Pooja just made to me and how could she say so knowing Pooja well. Till now I had seen only Raman adjusting in their married life.

"I am sick of you all," Pooja shouted and went inside her room banging the door.

"Here comes the next episode of our family drama." Nisha sarcastically remarked and went inside her room too.

Maa helplessly watched all this and she also left. I was still sitting there with her words getting louder and louder inside me.

I opened the mail which Himakshi had sent me three years before. I could neither have the courage to see it nor delete it, till now. But today I wanted to see it, I wanted to see Vaibhav.

Himakshi had sent me the pictures of Vaibhav's wedding. I too had received his invitation but could not go as Maa was not well. Perhaps even if she was fine, I could not have mustered the courage to go, to watch his wife taking the place I wanted to have, the place he wanted to give me.

I searched for her mail with the subject line

'See what you have missed in your life'. Vaibhav looked stunning in his wedding *sherwani* and his bride looked beautiful. Her *chura, sindoor, mangalsutra* everything was so pretty and all this could have been mine. I pictured myself standing there, in place of her, in that crimson red lehenga, with Vaibhav's hand over my shoulder.

I closed my eyes. I could neither stop my tears nor Himakshi's warnings, echoing inside me.

I knew she was right but I had to give that chance to my family. But now, the saturation point had come or it had come long back and I failed to see it. I needed to fix this now because it's better late than never.

The next morning, I went to Pooja's room. It was 10.30 am and she was still sleeping. Nisha was watching TV and Maa was preparing food in the kitchen.

"Pooja, get up. We need to talk."

"Mmm, let me sleep. Even here I can't sleep peacefully."

"Get up. Let us talk and then you can sleep

for as long as you want." I had never been that stern with her before. Had I been, things could have been better.

"OK, tell me. What happened," my changed tone made her sit up."

"Freshen up. I am waiting for you in my room."

She got up grumping and minutes later was in my room. Maa also sensed something and came along with her.

"Come Maa, I need you to stay here."

"What's the matter?" Pooja was baffled now.

"What have you decided?" I asked, looking straight into her eyes.

"Decided for what?"

"I spoke to Raman last night. He told me you are thinking of separating with him."

Maa was surprised to know this.

"It's my personal matter. I will see what I have to do." Pooja, as usual, rudely replied.

"You better sort your personal matters at your home. If it's in my house, it's not your personal anymore," I raised my voice.

I am not sure if it was my unusual high pitch or straightforward words that caught Nisha's attention and she joined the room too.

"What do you mean? Is this not my house? See Maa, how is Di talking to me."

Maa tried to say something but chose to keep mum.

"Pooja, if you have trouble with your husband or in-laws, I can talk to them and if you want to reconcile, I am there to help you. Even if you think you cannot survive in that marriage, that's also fine by me. After all, it's your life, but do not assume you can simply pile up here."

"Pile up? Am I piling up? Do girls pile up when they visit their home after marriage? I am already suffering in my marriage and now this? Had Dad been alive today..."

"ENOUGH!!" My rage was uncontrollable now. Pooja almost shivered.

"Had he been alive, you would have got your lessons long back. He would never have tolerated your rubbish." I closed my eyes to stop my tears. I didn't want to fall weak at this moment. "When we lost him, I tried my best to take that role for you both but that needed reciprocation too. But it was all my mistake. I loved you both more than myself and I allowed you to take me for granted. Anyways, now it's time that I rectify my mistake. You have a week's time to decide and look for alternate accommodation for yourself."

"Di, how can you do this? You are throwing a married girl out of her house. Do you have any idea what it means?"

"No, I don't have any idea because I could not get married. But I have a much better idea than you in dealing with relationships, in bearing responsibilities, and in being reliable. I don't need the label of being married to prove my worth to anyone. So, you better stop this 'married thing' with me." It was getting hard to control my tears now.

"But Beta, where will she go?" Maa came close to me and said in a meek tone.

"She is educated and intelligent, Maa. She can sort out her problems," I knew Maa was not happy with my answer. "When I can start from almost scratch without any support, she can manage well too. If she needs any help, I am there but she has to earn that help first."

I turned over to Pooja, "Think over it and if you decide to separate from your husband, start looking for alternate accommodation. You may leave now."

I don't know whether Maa agreed with my decision or not but she didn't retaliate either.

Pooja was even more agonised but now I did not care. Nisha was probably trying to believe what she just saw. And Maa stood there as a silent spectator just the way she always did.

I waited for a long time for her to take that stand for me. But I learnt it. If I won't stand for myself, no one else will.

'Announcement: The next station is Punjabi Bagh West.'

The announcement made me open my eyes. I wiped my tears and looked up to her.

She seemed even more graceful now.

"You were right. These women around me definitely deserve bravery awards. They deserve huge rounds of applause."

I took a deep sigh.

"I missed my Kirti Nagar station too. So.."

I was waiting for the compartment's response. "Hello, what next?" I didn't get any answer. "Hello..."

Still nothing. "Heyy, talk to me. You can't get quite like this. Talk to me." I got impatient and didn't realize I was speaking out loud. "C'mon, speak out."

I felt a hand on my shoulder. "Are you OK, beta? Do you need any help?" An elderly woman sitting beside me asked with concern.

I composed myself. I picked up my bag and got up to leave.

What was this? Was I day-dreaming? Have I gone crazy? I stood near the door and was waiting for it to open. The train was about to halt when I heard it again.

"You forgot to take that book."

"Hey," I was so happy to hear its voice again.

"See you some other time, with some more stories. Bye."

I smiled, picked up my book and came out.

Everyday I board my train with the hope to catch that same compartment again. I am still waiting for that sound.

ABOUT THE AUTHOR

Parminder Kaur Sharma is a multifaceted personality. She is a Banker by profession, Engineer by qualification, and Writer by passion. She has both fiction and non-fiction books to her credit.

She is also a doting mother and an enthusiastic runner. She aims to create a positive impact in the lives of her readers through her writing.

www.parminderkaursharma.com
Email: author.parminderksharma@gmail.com

AFTERWORD

Thank you for reading this book. This is my second book and it has taken a lot of effort to pen this down.

The people and incidents around us teach us very important lessons for life. The aim behind writing this book is to motivate the readers to fight their battles with character and poise.

I hope I have done justice in portraying the different characters of the stories.

I would be delighted to hear your review. Would you mind spending a minute to share your experience while reading this book? Did you like reading it and if yes, which character and which story you liked the most?

Your feedback matters to me!

ALSO FROM THE AUTHOR

Are you struggling with your child's tantrums or child bullying or want to know ways to engage a hyperactive child or wonder how to make your child a better and effective learner? Then this book is for you.

http://mybook.to/FMTP

It also serves to deal with the indirect partners of parenting- your relationship with your husband, your mother-in-law, your child's teacher and of course your own self.

Bonus : Ten tried and tested tips!

www.ingramcontent.com/pod-product-compliance
Lightning Source LLC
Chambersburg PA
CBHW062137160726
48282CB00027B/859
9789354932588